Chris glanced around to see if anyone was watching them. No one was.

He carried the package into his little room and closed the door. There he inspected it again and turned it over to see if Mike's teeth had damaged the other side. He hoped the contents had not been damaged. He shook the box and listened for the rattle of broken glass or something.

A thin film of white powder trickled out the holes Mike's teeth had made. He shook a little into his hand and looked at it. It was as fine as talcum powder. Powdered sugar. Why would anyone send a package of powdered sugar through the mail? He wet a finger, touched it to the powder and tasted it. Then he just stood there, his face twisted out of shape, and shock rolled through him in waves. What he had just tasted was heroin.

MORE PAGE-TURNING ADVENTURES
FROM PUFFIN!

Hero

by Walt Morey

PUFFIN BOOKS

PUFFIN BOOKS
Published by the Penguin Group
Penguin Books USA Inc., 375 Hudson Street, New York, New York 10014, U.S.A.
Penguin Books Ltd, 27 Wrights Lane, London W8 5TZ, England
Penguin Books Australia Ltd, Ringwood, Victoria, Australia
Penguin Books Canada Ltd, 10 Alcorn Avenue, Toronto, Ontario, Canada M4V 3B2
Penguin Books (N.Z.) Ltd, 182-190 Wairau Road, Auckland 10, New Zealand

Penguin Books Ltd, Registered Offices: Harmondsworth, Middlesex, England

First published in the United States of America under the title *The Lemon Meringue Dog* by
E.P. Dutton, 1980
Published in Puffin Books, 1995

10 9 8 7 6 5 4 3 2 1

LIBRARY OF CONGRESS CATALOGING-IN-PUBLICATION DATA
Morey, Walt.
Hero / by Walt Morey.
p. cm.
Previously titled: The lemon meringue dog.
Summary: When former Coast Guardsman Chris George and his drug-sniffing dog Mike
stumble upon a package of heroin, they draw the attention of some sinister characters.
ISBN 0-14-037793-x
[1. Police dogs—Fiction. 2. Narcotics, Control of—Fiction.] I. Title.
PZ7.M816He 1995 [Fic]—dc20 95-19681 CIP AC

Printed in the United States of America

To Chris Fesler,
without whose help this book
could not have been written.

Hero

1

Chris stood at the edge of the dock and watched an oceangoing tug nudge a rust-streaked freighter into her berth. Three men and a large brown German shepherd dog were with him, but he had never felt more alone.

Before him the bay stretched flat and shining, running outward to join the distant sea. Behind him rows of warehouses lined the dock. Beyond the warehouses the city rose tier on tier into the blue sky, blanketing the surrounding hills and making this one of the great ports of the world. A gull lit on a nearby piling and surveyed the little group with bright black eyes.

One was a Coast Guard lieutenant. Two were Coast Guard personnel with rifles and pistols. Chris was also a coastguardsman and, at twenty, the youngest. He was slender, with straight blond hair and mild blue, worried eyes. He licked his dry lips nervously and watched the freighter move in. He held the leash of the dog and kept him close beside him. The dog whined nervously and pressed against his legs. Every minute or two his front paws did an excited little dance.. Chris patted his head and murmured, "It's all right, Mike. Be quiet. Just be quiet." Each time, the dog licked his hand and was still for a moment.

Lieutenant Ballard frowned and said, "Keep that animal quiet, sailor. And you calm down too. You're jittery as a grasshopper on a hot stove. Relax. There's nothing to worry about."

"It's my first time, sir," Chris said. "It's Mike's too."

Lieutenant Ballard grunted, annoyed. He was a lean, tough career man with more than twelve years in the service. "You've been training for this five months now," he pointed out. "It's no big thing. It's just another exercise like dozens of others you've been through."

"Yes sir," Chris said. But it wasn't. During all those months of training, there'd never been men with guns backing him up, ready to use them. Not once had he boarded a strange ship, where unknown men who'd broken the law also had guns they were prepared to use.

It had been common knowledge for a long time that somehow foreign drugs were coming into the city and, from here, fanning out all over the country. All law enforcement agencies had instituted programs to try to stop the traffic. The Coast Guard, responsible for the harbor and all arriving and departing ships, set up its own program. They began training dogs to sniff out drugs, and men to handle them.

Chris applied for admittance to the program and was accepted. After all, he was a farm boy and had been around animals all his life. As a handler he was considered a natural.

They gave him Mike to work with. The first time they met, Mike reared against his chest, and their eyes met just a foot away. Chris patted the big head and knew that here was an animal of exceptional intelligence. And so Mike proved to be.

The other handlers worked all day teaching their dogs to perform some task. Mike got it sometimes on the third or fourth try. He watched Chris, sharp ears pricked forward, big head tipped sideways as if to say "Show me. I can do it." And he always could. The man overseeing their training observed one day that "Mike's doing a pretty good job training you, sailor." Chris agreed that he was.

Chris and Mike were together almost every waking hour. Chris was responsible for the big dog. He fed him, bathed him. They worked and played together. They soon became the best team in the Coast Guard's drug-bust pilot program. Their performance was swift and Mike's delicate nose was deadly accurate. Not once did he miss a hidden packet of drugs.

Chris heard Captain Wilson was pleased and surprised. Pleased with Mike's performance, surprised at Chris's because he was the youngest in the program and he didn't have the tough appearance and approach to the job of the others. Mike alone earned them their good reputation as a team. Chris gave his whole love to the big dog as he'd never given it to any other living thing. And Mike, raised in a kennel and with no close association with anyone like Chris, responded.

A reliable tip came in that forty pounds of pure heroin was to be smuggled into the country through this port. It was supposed to be hidden aboard this grubby, rusty freighter, the *Coral Queen,* that was now being nudged into the dock.

Chris and Mike were here to try to find it. It was their first real test. It was the Coast Guard's initial unveiling of their drug-bust program. Chris didn't know why Mike should have butterflies in his stomach, too. But the big dog was smart and sensitive. Somehow in his dog brain, he knew and was reacting.

The freighter was finally snugged in against the dock, the gangplank run out, and they went aboard. The captain, a burly, scowling man with a stained captain's cap perched on the back of his head, barred their way at the top of the gangplank. A pair of ship's officers, as tough looking as the captain, flanked him. "What's the Coast Guard doing boarding my ship, and with weapons?" the captain demanded.

Lieutenant Ballard explained quietly, "Drugs have been coming into the country through this port, captain. We're trying to stop it. Our job is to search every arriving ship. There's nothing personal."

"Then why pick on me?" the captain complained. "There's a thousand other ways for dope to get into the

4

country: cars, trucks, planes, people carrying it, to name a few. I say it's mighty personal."

"Every means in and out of the city is being checked, captain. The Coast Guard's part is to search every ship entering and leaving the harbor."

"Them, too?" the captain pointed toward several freighters moored farther down the dock.

"Those, too, if there seems to be a reason."

"You're saying you've got a reason for boarding me, lieutenant. I don't like it. You show up here with guns and a dope-sniffing dog, as if you expected to find something. I can tell you nothing comes aboard this ship that I don't know about."

"Then you've no objection to our looking, captain?"

The captain scowled and rubbed his jaw angrily.

Ballard said quietly, "I can get all the authority I need, captain. But I'd rather not do that."

"That sounds like a threat," the captain said.

"It's not meant that way. Everybody gets the same treatment. That's how it has to be."

The captain's scowl became blacker. The hand caressing his chin balled into a fist. After a tense minute he shrugged. "All right, lieutenant, help yourself. But my men and I are coming along."

"I hope you do." Ballard turned to Chris. "All right, sailor, let's get on with this."

None of their training had been aboard an actual ship, so Chris took a minute to decide where to begin. The top deck, he decided, as high as he could go and work down a deck at a time.

Followed by Lieutenant Ballard, the two men with

weapons, the ship's captain and his officers, Chris led Mike to the top deck. There he hesitated again and looked the length of the ship. It was half again as long as a football field and was littered with coiled chains, lines, pipes running every direction, and hundreds of nooks and corners. Dope could be hidden anywhere. And the decks below would be even harder to search, because of the countless beehive compartments. They had only to overlook one small spot to miss it. Even for a dog with Mike's supersensitive nose, this was a mountainous problem.

Annoyed, Ballard said, "Come on, sailor, let's get with it."

"Yes, sir." Chris patted Mike's broad head and said, "All right, Mike. Find it! Find it!"

Mike set off just as he had during the months of training, tail waving, head down, delicate black nose twitching as he poked it into holes and corners, dark nooks, and pipe ends. He inspected coils of rope and chain and thrust his nose under a tarp, stretched over cargo lashed to the deck. He even forced his nose under the covering over the lifeboats and sniffed loudly. He was doing an excellent job. If there was anything here, Mike's nose would find it, Chris thought proudly. His confidence returned.

As he'd been taught, Chris held a reasonably short leash. This gave Mike freedom of movement, and yet Chris could control his area of search. He made sure that Mike missed no promising-looking spots. Heroin could be in one big package, but more likely it would be broken down into a number of small ones.

Mike traveled fast. Sometimes Chris almost ran to keep up. The rest of the party was strung out behind them.

They completely combed the upper deck, and Mike found nothing. It had taken but a few minutes.

They dropped down one deck and Mike went to work again. Here the compartments were small, close together. There were lockers, cupboards, furniture of all kinds, and rows and rows of shelves and lockers to be inspected. Here in the inner confines, the countless aromas of the ship were trapped. The companionways were narrow. The short leash put Mike at a disadvantage. It restricted his freedom of movement. Chris was practically tramping on the dog's heels and destroying his concentration. Chris let out the leash to its full length, and they promptly got into more trouble. The extra length let Mike dash into a compartment, ahead of Chris. He got tangled up in furniture and had to wait for Chris to free him, or he passed on one side of a table or chair, while Chris went the other way. Chris finally unhooked the leash and turned Mike loose.

Mike was off. He whipped into and out of compartments. He climbed over furniture, desks, bunks or any other obstruction, his black nose working. Chris had no idea he could move so fast. Sometimes he almost ran to keep up, especially when Mike headed for another open door.

They had progressed almost halfway down a companionway, when Mike shot out of a compartment and stopped dead. His head came up. His nose pointed down the companionway. His sharp ears jerked forward expectantly. His whole body was tensely alert. Chris knew what was coming, and his heart jumped into his throat. This was the way Mike always acted when he spotted the package that had been hidden during practice. Mike took off down the companionway and whipped out of sight through an open door.

'"He's found it!" Chris said excitedly and began to run.

Chris was still several steps from the door when he heard the crash. He dashed into the compartment and stopped in horror. "No! No!" he said aghast. "Oh, no!" Those following piled up in the doorway behind him.

They were in the galley. Mike stood in the center of the wreckage of a lemon meringue pie, contents splashed across the floor. He looked up, happily waving his tail, his face smeared from the tip of his nose to his eyes with gobs of dripping lemon meringue. He licked his lips gleefully and went back to gobbling the pie.

Chris knew what had happened. Mike had a sweet tooth, and he especially loved lemon meringue pie. Chris had discovered this the first week they were together. Lemon meringue was his own favorite pie. One day he had a piece for lunch and Mike stood before him, big eyes grudging him every bite, licking his lips hopefully. Chris finally gave him a piece, and he so obviously loved it that, from then on, the dog always got at least half of his helping of pie. This pie was fresh from the oven, and Mike's sensitive nose had picked up the mouth-watering aroma out in the companionway. He'd made straight for the galley where he reared up, knocked the pie off the counter, and went happily to work.

"Oh, no, Mike! No! No!" He dove for Mike's collar to drag him out of the gooey mess. He got hold of the collar, but his sudden movement startled the dog. Mike jerked away. Chris was overbalanced and was yanked over on his back. He clung to Mike's collar and was dragged through the meringue, scrambling frantically to turn over and get his feet under him. The pie filling and meringue were like grease. He kept panting, "Stop it, Mike! Stop it, you hear?" Finally he got turned over, jerked Mike close, and threw an arm around his neck to hold him still. Mike kept struggling to get back to the counter. Chris cuffed his ears and said sharply, "Cut that out! That's enough!" He grabbed a towel off the counter and wiped the meringue from Mike's face and his own hands.

Lieutenant Ballard and the little group of men watched silently. When he finished, Chris said hastily, "I'm sorry, sir. It won't happen again. It—it was an accident. You see, Mike has a sweet tooth. He smelled this pie and he likes lemon meringue and . . ."

"Knock off the alibis, sailor." Ballard's face was flushed, his voice deadly with barely controlled anger. "I'm not interested."

The captain said, "Lieutenant, I've put up with this so-called boarding party of yours practically taking over my ship without even a 'by-your-leave,' but it just seems to me I don't have to tolerate this very bad amateur comedy."

Lieutenant Ballard's lips were tight. "I agree with you, captain." He said to Chris in an icy voice, "Get that clown out of here, sailor. Get him out before I shoot him."

"But, sir . . ." Chris began.

"I mean now." Ballard turned to one of the armed men. "Take them back to the base and bring out another dog and handler. We'll wait."

Chris said desperately, "It won't happen again, sir. It was my fault. If you'll just let us finish . . ."

"I said get him out of here."

Chris knew what an unforgivable tragedy this was, and he had to try to rectify it at all cost. "He was doing fine, sir. He wants to go back to work right now. You can see he does. Let him, lieutenant. I promise it won't happen again."

The lieutenant leaned forward, his sharp features livid. "That's right, it won't. Now get out of here, both of you. And you, sailor, are confined to quarters until further notice."

"Yes, sir." Chris rose then. He snapped the leash on Mike and dragged him out and off the freighter. One of the armed men followed, put them in the back of the Coast Guard van, and drove back to the base.

At the base, Chris returned Mike to the kennel. There he knelt and took the dog's big head in his hands. They'd gone out to the ship to perform a very serious duty and, as the ship's captain said, it had

10

turned into very low comedy on the galley floor. Since this was the first time the Coast Guard's drug-bust program had been used, it had made it much worse.

"It's all right," he told Mike. "It wasn't your fault. It was mine all the way. If I just hadn't given you that first bite of pie, this would never have happened."

Mike knew something was wrong. He licked Chris's face and whined anxiously.

"I'm sorry," Chris said. "I really messed us both up."

He patted Mike's head again. Then he closed the gate and left.

Chris felt sick. They had both failed miserably on their first try. He didn't know what would happen to them now. But knowing Lieutenant Ballard as he did, he was sure it would not be pleasant.

2

The impersonal blare of the PA system sounded like the voice of doom. "Shore Patrolman third class Christopher George report to Captain Wilson's office immediately."

Chris knew what that order meant. He would not be court-martialed for yesterday's happening as he feared. But he would face the closest thing to it, a captain's mast. Captain Wilson would be the sole judge. That could be almost as bad as a court-martial. Captain Wilson was a wide-shouldered, big-chested man with iron grey hair. The Coast Guard was his life. He lived by its rules and expected everyone else to. He was very tough, but the talk on the base was that he was fair. A ball of apprehension settled in Chris's stomach as he hurried toward the captain's office.

Lieutenant Ballard and the two weapons-carrying men were there. No one spoke to Chris.

12

He faced Captain Wilson across the big desk. The captain's grey eyes were direct and cool, his voice impersonal. "You know why you're here?"

"Yes, sir," Chris said.

Captain Wilson leaned his elbows on the desk. "Shore Patrolman third class George," he said, "you are charged with violation of Article 42, in that you either willfully or unknowingly discharged your duties in an unlawful manner yesterday afternoon. Do you understand these charges?"

"Yes, sir," Chris said.

Article 42 was a charge that could cover almost anything and it was often used when no specific charge was to be made.

Captain Wilson nodded to Lieutenant Ballard, "You may proceed, lieutenant."

The lieutenant had never liked Chris. From the very beginning he had tried to get Chris knocked out of the drug-bust program. He told Chris quite frankly, "This is a tough program, sailor. We need tough men. The people we're after are vicious Mafia characters who don't hesitate to kill. You simply don't look tough enough to me."

Chris asked quietly, "What do I look like to you, sir?"

"Frankly, like a kid fresh off the farm. If you got caught in a tight spot, I think you'd fold up on us. We can't have that. I'm giving you this chance to pull out on your own before you get washed out as unfit."

"Sir," Chris said in his most reasonable voice, "I was

chosen for this program because I passed all the requirements. I intend to try."

Chris tried especially hard. Mike and he became such a good team they were rated number one in the program, and thus he incurred Lieutenant Ballard's eternal enmity.

Lieutenant Ballard said now, "That dog, Mike"— and pointing at Chris—"and him, too. They made the whole boarding party look like a bunch of school-kid fools."

"How did he do that?" Captain Wilson asked.

"This was our first time out to show what we could do," Ballard said. "We should have looked real sharp and on our toes, so I took George, here, and his dog because they were number one in training. And what happened, sir? That dumb dog went for a lemon meringue pie, knocked it off the counter, and when we got there stood right in the middle of it, pie smeared all over his face, waving his tail and having the time of his life. The galley floor was a mess. To make it worse, George grabbed the dog and was dragged around in the goo, smearing meringue all over his uniform and turning the whole operation into the lowest kind of comedy. As if *that* wasn't enough, when I told George to get the dog out of there, he gave me a public argument."

"What sort of argument?"

"When I ordered him to take the dog out, he practically refused."

Captain Wilson held up a hand. "Hold it right there, lieutenant. Let's take this one step at a time." He looked at Chris. "You want to answer that?"

"I wasn't arguing, sir. I knew why Mike had gone after that pie." Very briefly Chris sketched for Captain Wilson how he had brought on Mike's addiction to lemon meringue pie. "You see, sir, it wasn't Mike's fault. It was mine. Yesterday when he smelled that fresh pie, he naturally thought it was for him. I thought he deserved another chance, sir. I still think so." Chris looked at Lieutenant Ballard. "He was doing fine until we got near the galley. Afterward he wanted to go back to work. You saw that, lieutenant."

"What I saw was a dog that had forgotten five months of training to eat pie," Ballard said spitefully. He turned to Captain Wilson. "That wasn't the worst part of it, sir. The replacement dog that we brought in found a small package of heroin buried in the bottom of a flour bin, within six feet of where that pie had been sitting."

"That proves what I just said," Chris said excitedly. "Mike smelled the heroin and was trying to get at it even while I held him."

"He could have smelled it when he first entered the galley," Ballard pointed out. "But he didn't."

Chris forgot he was in Captain Wilson's office to defend himself. He was fighting for Mike now. "I trained him for five months," he said hotly. "I say he spotted it while I was trying to hold him."

"Then he's not as good as everybody thought he

was," Ballard shot back. "The other dog found it the minute he entered the galley."

Chris had no answer to that. He looked anxiously at Captain Wilson, but that craggy face told him nothing. The captain said to the enlisted men, "Has either of you anything to add to this?"

Both shook their heads. One murmured, "It was just like the lieutenant said, sir."

Lieutenant Ballard said, "Captain, there is something else I think should be cleared up here."

"Very well, lieutenant," Captain Wilson said.

"You put me in charge of this pilot program, sir. I want it to be successful, so I need the best men on the base in it. I never thought Shore Patrolman George was fit for the program. I even told him that I thought he was too young and inexperienced, that he was better suited to milking cows and plowing fields than tracking down tough drug smugglers. I suggested he drop out. He refused, and against my better judgment I let him continue, figuring that he'd not be able to perform with the rest and would wash himself out. But he and that dog performed better than anyone else. It became a foregone conclusion that when our first big test came we'd use Shore Patrolman George and his dog."

"What are you getting at, lieutenant?"

"These drug people are very smart. They plan way ahead and they plan very carefully. There are no lengths they won't go to, to get a drug shipment in. I think they had it figured that George and his dog

16

would go out on our first search because he was number one in training. They got to him with a proposition."

Captain Wilson leaned back and looked at Ballard. "That's a mighty serious charge. Can you back it up?"

"I don't think George really knew what he was getting into," Ballard said quickly. "I'm suggesting that he's just gullible enough to let them use him, without fully realizing what he was doing. I doubt that forty pounds of heroin was ever on board. They set that up as a trial run, so they could see how we conducted a search and who would do it. How they convinced him there was no real harm in what they'd have him do, I don't know. But somehow they did it. The ship's captain and his officers were with us every minute, watching. I think George's pay for cooperating with them would have been that six-ounce-or-so package we found."

"That's a lie," Chris burst out. "The whole thing is lies."

"You just wait a minute," Captain Wilson said. "You'll get your turn." He turned to Lieutenant Ballard again. His voice was tough. "You've obviously done some thinking on this. Spell it out just how you think it was done."

"I figure the whole thing was staged and George helped set it up. He told the captain how the dog would go for lemon meringue pie. In the search he, George, had to miss that package. To do it, he had to momentarily destroy the dog's sense of smell. What better, more logical way, one that could be easily arranged, than that piece of lemon meringue pie sitting on the drainboard? It has a reasonably strong, sweet odor and the lemon meringue is sticky and will cling to the dog's nose.

"George was supposed to keep the dog on leash at all times. On the upper deck he did. As soon as we got below, where the galley was, he turned him loose. Why? I think, so he could rush into the galley ahead of everybody and knock that pie off the counter and get his face smeared with it. After the search had turned up nothing, George could either return for that six-ounce package of heroin or somebody could deliver it to him."

Captain Wilson rubbed his chin thoughtfully and said nothing.

Lieutenant Ballard said, "That package is worth about eighteen thousand dollars street value, sir. That's pretty good pay for doing so little."

"That's crazy," Chris exploded. "Why would I get mixed up in something like that?"

"That's a good question, lieutenant," Captain Wilson said.

Ballard looked full at Chris, obviously enjoying what he was about to say. "You bought an old run-down farm a few miles out about a year ago. You still owe ten thousand dollars on it." He turned to Captain Wilson. "That's common knowledge here on the base, sir. I did a little further checking on my own and discovered there's a lot of back taxes due. In fact, so much that the county will foreclose and sell it for taxes unless it's paid this year. Those taxes come to better than fifteen hundred dollars. That heroin would pay up the back taxes and pick up the mortgage and leave a few thousand over."

"Is that correct, sailor?" Captain Wilson asked.

"I'll have the tax money this fall. I'll take care of it."

"But you did buy a place you're in debt for, and the county is about to foreclose on you?"

"Yes, sir, that part's true. The rest isn't."

"For your information, sailor, I've done research on these drug people and the way they operate," Ballard said. "They're very ingenious. Something that would normally seem farfetched is logical with them."

Captain Wilson cut in to ask Chris, "You're saying it was not the way the lieutenant described it?"

"It went off just as he described it," Chris admitted. "But not for the reasons he gave. He read into what happened yesterday, things that aren't true. The lieutenant and I have never hit it off, for the reasons he gave. That's why I worked so hard to be the best."

"Why did you want in the drug-bust program?" the Captain asked.

It was on the tip of Chris's tongue to blurt out that he'd never been anything. In school, he was just an average student who made few friends. He had to hurry home every night to do chores, on the hundred-acre farm where he lived with an uncle and aunt. For seven years he was another pair of hands to milk, to run a tractor, to do all the things that had to be done

seven days a week. He had no feeling of family or relatives. He had a place to board but no home. He didn't
even own the clothes on his back. He belonged no-
where and to no one. He could put down no roots. He
was nothing. When his uncle and aunt sold out and
retired, there was no place to go. Another boy suggested the Coast Guard. It was a good place to learn a
trade. He joined.

For three years he was just another enlisted man.
Then one·day he rented a car and drove out to look at
the old place where he'd lived. He never got there.

A mile from the house a For Sale sign was nailed to
a tree in front of a small farm. He knew the Millers, a
retired couple living out their years. The place was
about ten acres with a creek. The buildings were old.
They had a tractor and a few tools, a couple of
hundred chickens and a cow. He passed the place
every day going to school, and he'd always been drawn
to it and the possibilities he could see. He stopped to
talk with them.

The Millers wanted to go East to their son. They
wanted ten thousand, and the buyer would have to
pick up the back taxes—a few hundred dollars. They
had just put up the sign. It was a buy. It would not
last long. Chris had saved a little money. He signed a
contract they had that afternoon.

Afterward, Chris stood in the road in front of the
place and looked at it. He told himself it was his. By
golly, he owned it! He was a landowner, a man of
property! Now he could put down roots. He belonged

someplace. He was somebody! In all his life he had never known such a feeling of worth.

The first of the year, Chris learned that the back taxes were fifteen hundred dollars. They hadn't been paid in years. He had this year to make it all up or lose the place. The drug-bust program came along just in time. He tried for it because it meant an increase in rank and pay and he needed that extra money. He looked into Captain Wilson's stony face and said, "I wanted in because I needed the extra money."

"To meet your obligations?"

"Yes, sir," Chris said. He knew he had walked right into a trap.

Captain Wilson tapped the end of a pencil on the desk and asked idly, "When did you first meet Captain Norton?"

"I don't know a Captain Norton, sir."

"He's captain of the *Coral Queen,* the freighter you were on yesterday."

"I never saw him before yesterday. I didn't meet him then or even speak to him. He was just there. That's all I know about him."

"I see." But watching the captain, toying idly with a pencil and frowning darkly, Chris knew the man didn't believe him. Finally Captain Wilson tossed the pencil aside, leaned back and fixed Chris with a drilling look. "If I could prove even half these accusations, I'd boot you out of the service with a dishonorable discharge. To say the least, your conduct yesterday was amateurish and slipshod. You were no credit to the drug

21

program or the service. Putting aside some very strong suspicions, I have decided to impose the following sentence. Reduction to the next inferior pay grade, loss of rank and return to your last rate of yeoman. Report to the personnel officer for assignment immediately. That's all."

Chris started to leave, then turned back. "Sir, what will happen to Mike, to the dog?"

Captain Wilson said, "He's obviously unreliable. We'll sell him, try to recover some of the money that's been invested in him."

Chris left and Lieutenant Ballard followed him outside. "You ruined a good dog, sailor. I hope you know it. The captain was mighty lenient with you. He could have booted you out. I would have. You knew where that heroin in the galley was, all right. I think you know where that forty pounds is, too."

"Then you didn't find it?" Chris asked.

"You know we didn't, sailor." With that Ballard walked off.

On his way to report to the personnel officer, Chris detoured to pass the dog run. Mike was the only one there. He reared against the wire, whining and waving his tail. Chris put his hands through the wire, patted his head, and scratched his sharp ears. "I'm sorry," he said. "I wish I knew some way to tell you how sorry I am. It was your being so smart that made me look good. Don't think I don't know it. If I just hadn't let you have that pie. Maybe the lieutenant's right, and all I'm good for is milking cows."

Then he remembered Mike was to be sold. He'd never see him again, never feel his warm tongue licking his hand as if he understood. He wouldn't have those intelligent eyes studying him, as if to say "Just show me what you want. I'll do it." The close companionship they'd known these past months was ended.

Chris wondered what the person who bought Mike would be like. Would he be good to him? Where would he take Mike? Would he take the trouble to understand the dog and feed him properly? Would he exercise him, talk to him, play with him, and love him as Chris had? Chris gave full play to all these thoughts, and when he finished he knew he could not let some stranger have Mike. By every rule of love, devotion and need, Mike belonged to him. If Mike was going to be sold, then he had to try to buy him.

He couldn't go to Captain Wilson. The captain was in no mood to do him any favors. Someone else had to do that for him. Someone who had access to the captain and to whom Wilson would listen. There was only one person who could do that. The chaplain, Reverend Holloway, carried more weight than anyone on the base. He would stop by Chaplain Holloway's on the way to personnel.

Chaplain Holloway was a small, round man with a pleasant smile and an almost completely bald head. He sat in his living room, small hands folded in his lap, and listened to Chris's plea. When Chris finished he said, "Now let me understand this. You want me to intercede on your behalf with Captain Wilson to make it possible to buy Mike, the dog?"

Chris nodded. "He'll listen to you. He won't to me."

"Have you considered the consequences of buying this dog, Chris?"

"I'll save Mike from being bought by some stranger who maybe won't take good care of him."

"That's not what I mean. That dog cost a lot of money to begin with. Then the government paid for five months of training. They're going to try to get as much of it back as possible. Mike could cost you five or six hundred dollars. Maybe more. Is Mike worth that much to you?"

Chris could not explain to Chaplain Holloway how it was with Mike and him. Mike was more than just a big friendly dog he happened to love. He was all the friends, the family he'd never had. He was all the pets he had never been able to have on the farm, because his uncle looked upon animals as something to sell or send to the butcher. Mike trusted him completely. He depended upon Chris for love, and food and care. He was the only living thing Chris had ever felt totally responsible for. If he bought Mike, it could mean he'd not raise the money for the delinquent taxes and he'd lose the farm. He wanted it. But Mike was a living, breathing, loving companion. He could get another farm. He wanted Mike more.

He said to the chaplain, "It'll take most of what I've managed to save. But I can't let Mike go to somebody else."

24

"You understand that once you've bought him, you've just started to spend."

"How is that?"

"You can't keep him in the barracks with you. You'll have to board him at some kennel, which is expensive. Or if you want to keep him with you, you'll have to find someplace to rent and live off the base. Rent is very high. It'll take a big chunk of your paycheck, and places that will let you keep a big dog like Mike are scarce. You'll have to buy all the feed for Mike. It'll cost almost as much to feed him as it will a person. And any way you figure it, once you live off the base, you'll be eating a lot of meals in restaurants, or buying your own food. Neither one is cheap. About seventy percent of your wages will go for rent and food for you and Mike. It's something to consider, Chris."

Chris hadn't thought about it. He did now. Then he said, "I'll have to get another job. I'll moonlight."

"An eight-hour shift here on the post and another somewhere else makes a long day," Holloway suggested.

"Can you think of any other way?" And when Holloway shook his head, "Then I have to do it. I've only got ten more months to go and I'm out. I've a good job waiting for me with an electrical firm. I can hold down an outside job for four or five months," Chris reasoned. "That should give me enough extra money to see me through to the end of my enlistment."

Holloway shook his head. "All for a dog you don't need. You're not making much sense, Chris. I know

25

you're attached to the animal and don't want to see him go to someone else. But you needn't worry. The Coast Guard will see that he gets a good home."

"It's more than that," Chris said. "I have to have Mike. I guess nobody'd understand that."

Holloway smiled. "Maybe I understand more than you think. All right, Chris, I'll do what I can. I'll talk with Captain Wilson but I can't promise it will do much good. As far as selling the dog is concerned, I imagine it will be first come as long as it's a responsible person."

"I'll have to find a place to move," Chris said, "and begin looking for some kind of outside job."

"One thing at a time, sailor," Holloway said. "If you get the dog, then we'll begin looking for someplace to stay, and if you find a room or apartment, then we'll begin looking for a job."

"Awful lot of ifs," Chris said.

"That's what I've been trying to tell you. Now, how high can you afford to go to buy the dog?"

"I've got almost eight hundred dollars in the bank," Chris said.

"It could take most of it. Do you want to get him if it does?"

Chris could see now that he wasn't going to be able to put by any money to save the farm anyway. It was already lost, so what difference did it make? He nodded. "Even if it takes it all," he said.

Holloway nodded. "I'll do my best for you. What's your new assignment here on the base?"

"I'm going to personnel now to find out."

"Check with me when you get off. I should have something."

The personnel officer's name was Sullivan. He grinned at Chris and said, "So you're back. I hear you and your dog put on quite a show yesterday." When Chris just looked at him, he became busy and said, "Let's see, you were in the mail room before. Right? You can go back there beginning right now, yeoman."

He was back where he'd started three years before.

Chris sorted mail the rest of the day. The personnel on the post came and went. Some looked a little surprised at seeing him here again, but nothing was said. It was obvious the whole base knew what had happened. He didn't care, if he could just get Mike. He thought about that all day and could hardly wait to get off.

The moment he was off, he hurried to find Chaplain Holloway. "Well," the little chaplain greeted him, "you've got Mike. He cost you six hundred dollars. I'm sorry I couldn't get him any cheaper. Now you have to leave him in a boarding kennel or find someplace off the base to live. Whichever, you'll have to hurry. Captain Wilson will let you keep Mike here for only another three days. I had to talk like a Dutch uncle to get that concession. Now, have you anything lined up in the way of a second job and a place to stay?"

"No," Chris said, "I'll begin looking right away."

"I'll keep an eye out too," Chaplain Holloway said. Chris tried to thank him and the little man smiled. "All part of the job, sailor."

Chris had gone straight from living on the farm into

the Coast Guard. He had no idea how hard it was to find a place to live with a dog or how scarce jobs that fit his requirements were. He soon learned that renting was almost out of the question. The cost took his breath away. When he did find a place he might afford, they turned thumbs down on Mike. In the job department he had even worse luck. He combed the help wanted columns every day, but he was restricted to calling on them after work. Then he found others .had been there hours before. Any job worth taking was gone. The few he might have had a chance at wanted him during the hours he was on duty at the base.

The third day, Chris found a kennel to board Mike and moved him. It was expensive. He couldn't afford to keep him there long. He quit looking for a place to stay and concentrated on finding a job because he was going to need the money. Once he had the job, he could begin looking for someplace to live again.

For almost a week, Chris ran down every lead that sounded promising. He had no luck. In desperation he returned to Chaplain Holloway and asked him to intercede in his behalf with Captain Wilson once more, to get him transferred from the mail room to any kind of night work, so he'd have his days free to hunt an outside job. "He'll listen to you," Chris said. "He won't to me."

Holloway talked with Captain Wilson and reported back to Chris. "Not a chance. The captain is not exactly kindly disposed toward you, Chris. He says you're lucky you weren't kicked out of the service with a dishonorable discharge. I'm afraid I have to agree with him. Your conduct that day aboard the freighter wasn't exactly a credit to the Coast Guard and the drug program."

"You believe I deliberately staged that pie-eating incident?"

Chaplain Holloway shook his head. "Not at all. To me you're too naive to concoct such an elaborate plan, and if somehow you did, you'd look guilty as sin. No offense meant."

"I guess you're right," Chris agreed ruefully. "Why couldn't Captain Wilson and Lieutenant Ballard see that in me?"

"They're hard-headed military men. You made the Coast Guard look bad and therefore made them look bad. They're in no mood to look for reasons why you're innocent. They took it personally. In a way it's tougher on the lieutenant. He is heading up the program."

Two days later, Chris had just got off duty and was heading out to run down a pair of promising leads when he met Chaplain Holloway hurrying toward him. The Chaplain was smiling. "I was hoping to catch you before you got away," he said.

Chris sensed immediately he had good news. "You've found me a job?"

"Better than that." Holloway lifted a chubby finger, pointing toward the blue sky for emphasis. "Somebody up there was with me today. I found a job *and* a place to live."

"That's marvelous!" Chris was excited. "Where's the job and where do I live?"

"The job is the central post office. The big one down on the waterfront. A friend of mine was night watchman there, the 'door rattler' he called it, from four until midnight. He quit and the job was open. The fact you have a trained German shepherd is really what got you the job. It's a tough area of the city. Somebody is always throwing a rock through a window or trying to pick one of the outside locks or damaging one of the mail trucks or something. They figure that the dog will be a real deterrent. There'll be people working there, sorting mail and such, all night. Your and Mike's job will be that of a night watchman. There are a lot of mail trucks and such in the lot. You'll have to guard them and check over the building every hour or so. They liked it that you work in the mail department on the base."

"That's marvelous!" Chris said happily. "Just marvelous! Now where do I live?"

"The greatest piece of luck of all." Chaplain Holloway was savoring his news and refused to be hurried. "Greatest piece of luck of all. Right out of the blue, so to speak, I was talking with some people and they mentioned that friends were going abroad for a year and were looking for someone to live in their house and take care of it. I told them about you. Once again they were especially interested in Mike. They figured that he would be an added protection. This is a houseboat on a small industry-deserted arm of the bay a

30

mile or so from the post office. There's about a hundred houseboats moored along an old wharf. They originally wanted two hundred dollars a month rent, but when I explained you were a serviceman with a trained guard dog, they dropped it to one fifty. Your watchman job will pay around three hundred dollars. With your Coast Guard pay you should be able to make it."

"I might even save a little," Chris said. "How soon can I go out there?"

"How long will it take to pack your seabag?"

"About ten minutes."

"I'll get my car. We'll pick up Mike and go right out."

The houseboat was tenth in a line of houseboats tied to the face of an old dock that was no longer used for commercial purposes. The houseboat was painted white, was box square and was built on a half dozen big logs. A porch ran completely around it. It was reached by a narrow wooden walkway suspended between swaying cables that stretched some seventy or eighty feet from the dock down to the porch. There were thirty or forty feet of open water between his houseboat and those on either side.

The walkway swayed as they went down. Mike whined nervously and pressed close against Chris. A pair of ducks, one with a bright green head, cruised from beneath the walkway. They looked up at the people above, quacked loudly, then went on toward the next houseboat, talking companionably.

There were four nicely furnished rooms and a bath. Chris said, "Gee! it's just like a real home."

"It is a real home," Chaplain Holloway said. "They expect you to care for it that way."

"I will," Chris said.

"You and Mike should do well here," Holloway said. "This arm of the bay is too shallow and narrow for big ships, so all you get is the pleasure-boat traffic. It'll be nice and quiet. You get off shift at the base at three. You're due at the post office at four. That gives you an hour to get down here, pick up Mike and get to work. Can you make it?"

"Easy," Chris said. "Mike and I thank you for all you've done for us."

Holloway smiled, "That's what they keep me around for. Well, I'll run along. Oh, the Careys left a lot of food in the refrigerator. You'd better eat it before it spoils."

When they were alone, Chris and Mike made a complete tour of the houseboat. It had a full bath, a nice bedroom and kitchen. The living room even had a fireplace. Mike stuck his nose into every corner of every room, tail waving happily. "Some diggings, huh?" Chris said. "What say we eat? I'm hungry."

The refrigerator was loaded. Chris prepared a good supper for Mike and himself. Afterward he took a chair out on the porch and with Mike lying at his feet they watched the last of the day drop behind the distant hills. The lights of the city came on. Night stretched a black curtain across the bay. The pair of ducks swam around the corner of the houseboat and cruised past, still talking. A gull planed out of the sky and landed without a ripple. A small yacht passed. The man at the wheel smiled and waved. A party of people walked the dock above. Their voices were a pleasant sound in the evening.

Chris thought about these last hectic days. He'd lost his rating, been kicked off the drug-bust program and had barely missed a dishonorable discharge. He had found a very nice place to live, found another job, and had acquired Mike. He had lost the farm. He was pretty sure of that. But it didn't matter. He let his hand trail over the side of the chair and touch Mike's sharp ears. He had Mike; that was most important. But, looking back, a lot of things had happened and all because of a piece of pie.

3

The first morning Chris left Mike alone in the houseboat, he gave the dog explicit instructions. "Now get this straight," he warned, holding Mike's big head in his hands and looking into his brown eyes. "This is no kennel. This is a home, a nice home. You remember that. I'm giving you the run of the house while I'm at the base. You take care of everything and don't start tearing up the carpet or the bed or knocking things on the floor."

Chris worried about Mike's behavior all day. The dog had never been in a house that he knew of. There was no telling what he might do. At three he left the base and hurried back to assess the damage, if any.

Mike had taken his instructions well. He was lying in the middle of the living room floor patiently waiting. A quick check showed not a thing had been disturbed.

Chris patted his head and said, "Good boy. You did fine. Now we can go to work."

The post office was an imposing, block-square structure of concrete, marble and glass four stories high. It was situated about three blocks from the bay, in an area of warehouses and truck terminals. It was a district to keep out of after dark. There were always stories in the paper of fights, muggings and break-ins.

A man from the postmaster's office showed Chris through the building and explained what he was to do. Mike trotted ahead of them at the very end of the leash, tail waving, acting important, as if he knew exactly what this was all about. "Glad you've got the dog," the man said. "Watchman needs one down here. Yours is the first we've ever had."

They began on the top floor. It was all offices. "These will be locked and vacant on your shift," he explained. "After eight or nine at night, put the run to anybody you find in these halls." The third floor was also offices, with a little sorting being done in a back room. The second and first floors were all sorting, with great lines of packages piled on long shelves and people sorting bags and piles of mail and putting them on trays. The trays were then put on four-wheeled carts, called pie carts, and delivered to designated spots.

The sorting area on the first floor was huge. A solid wall lined with hundreds of postal boxes separated it from the front where people came to transact business and pick up mail. A small ten-foot-square room off to one side was Chris and Mike's headquarters.

One whole side of the building was a block-long loading and unloading dock, lined with double doors. A dozen trucks were there handling bags of mail.

"This truck activity slacks off after about ten o'clock," the guide explained. "But keep a close watch on all these doors on this first floor and see that they're closed before you leave. We don't want any unauthorized people wandering around here. Check this floor every hour or so because of these doors and because it's the ground floor. That's about it. You and your dog will be pretty much on your own. I'll leave this whole building in your hands and Mike's paws." He smiled, patted Mike on the head, and left.

This was different from working in the mail room at the base. Here he had nothing to do with distribution, weighing, stamping, and sorting the thousands of pieces of mail that passed through the building every day. He seemed to have no particular boss.

Chris made his first tour in less than an hour. He wanted to get the feel of the place while everything was still fresh in his mind. He decided it was not necessary to keep Mike on a leash. The dog kept just a step or two ahead of him, as he'd been trained to do, head up, ears erect, and black nose twitching as it sucked in and catalogued all the strange smells. Chris smiled and said, "You don't have to look for dope here."

Workmen laughed and smiled. Some called to him or reached out to pat him as he trotted by. Good-natured comments followed them.

"Go get it, Mike. Find something, will you? A dog with your nose ought to find something even if it ain't here. We can all relax now, Mike's on the job."

Mike waved a friendly tail and went on about his business sniffing at packages, letters and boxes. At intervals, he reared up against a shelf or loaded pie cart and sniffed at parcels as if getting acquainted with their smells. Then he went on.

They checked out the interior of the first floor. Then, outside, they walked the length of the loading dock. Every one of the twenty doors was open, and a truck was backed up loading or unloading mail. They climbed the stairs to the second, third and fourth floors. When they finally returned to their own little room on the main floor, they had been gone a little more than an hour.

Chris decided to wait another half hour before making the next tour. Someone had left a sporting magazine on the table. He settled down to read an article about deer hunting. Mike stretched out on the floor beside him, put his big head on his paws, and went to sleep.

By ten o'clock the mail deliveries had slacked off. There were only four trucks at the unloading dock. The other doors were closed. He had to walk the length of the dock and check each one. This made the tour about fifteen minutes longer.

At midnight, when they went off shift, they had made five tours and Chris was ravenously hungry. He'd forgotten to bring a lunch. From now on, he'd put a couple of sandwiches in a paper bag the night before, along with something for Mike, and have them ready in the refrigerator.

The walk to the houseboat was about a mile along the old seawall that wound through an area of run-down warehouses, and businesses that barely scratched out an existence. Down here, at this time of night, Chris was glad he had Mike along. The whole length of the walk was lit only by a few small, bare light bulbs that burned above locked doors. There was one lighted business along the whole walk, a large commercial bakery, whose delicious smells drifted on the faint bay breeze. The front of the bakery had been turned into a retail store and quick-lunch counter to serve nearby workmen in factories and warehouses. Chris went in and sat down at the counter. Mike sat on his tail beside him, nose twitching, licking his lips at the enticing smells that filled the room.

The man behind the counter was big. He had a wrestler's chest and shoulders and thick arms. He wore a thin white shirt, the sleeves rolled high. There was a dusting of flour on his hands and fat face. A white baker's cap was pushed back on his round, bullet head. The word *Bruno* was printed on the cap.

Chris ordered a cup of coffee and a big round sugar doughnut. Bruno put them before him, leaned big arms on the counter and observed, "I know most everybody around here. I've never seen you before. You off a freighter or something?"

"I just started work at the post office. This was my first night. I'm sort of a guard."

"So old Dan Jackson finally retired. He's been threatening to. I never thought he would. He stopped in most every night after work. We got to be pretty good friends. He never had a dog though. How come they furnish you with a trained dog?"

"They didn't. He's mine. What makes you think he's a trained police dog?"

Bruno smiled. "I can spot one of these trained pooches about as far as I can see him. Their nose is always going a mile a minute, their eyes rolling around seeing everything, and their ears jumping back and forth. There's no mistaking a trained police dog. Okay if I pet him?"

"Of course," Chris said. "His name's Mike."

Bruno reached across the counter and patted Mike's big head. "You're quite a dog," he observed. "Don't tell me the post office is looking for robbers or dope or something? Jackson never said anything about any trouble."

Chris drank his coffee and said nothing.

Bruno laughed and slapped his shoulder. "Relax, boy, I wasn't trying to pry. I'm just a gabby guy, the night baker here. It gets mighty lonesome in this big old building, alone about this time of night. I rattle around like a single bean in a can. I think I'd be glad to talk to the devil himself." He glanced about almost distastefully, "It don't really pay to keep the place open past ten o'clock. But we do."

"Why?" Chris asked.

"One o'clock the trucks begin rolling in to load up for early morning deliveries to the stores. Somebody's got to be here. So"—he spread his thick arms—"I'm elected and we keep the joint open."

Chris felt foolish that for a moment he'd felt suspicious of this big, fat, good-natured man. There was no secret about where he worked or why or even the drug-bust program. Every law enforcement organization had its own program and everyone knew about it.

"There's nothing unusual about Mike and me," he ·said and told Bruno the whole story. When he finished, Bruno filled his coffee cup again and brought out another doughnut. "Here, give Mike a little treat. You've both had a tough break."

Bruno watched Chris break off chunks of doughnut and feed Mike and asked, "It's a pretty rough schedule you've laid out for yourself. You figure to keep it up indefinitely?"

"I've got about ten months to go until the end of my enlistment. I'd like to hold out until then."

"If anything should happen, come see me," Bruno offered. "Maybe I can put you on part time here. I need some help now and then."

Chris thanked him. Mike and he finished their coffee and doughnut and left.

That first evening established a set routine for the following nights: Stopping at the bakery, drinking coffee, and eating a doughnut while he talked with Bruno became habit.

A week later, Mike and he had just left the bakery when the dog looked back over his shoulder and his ears jumped forward. Chris glanced back along the dark, silent seawall and saw someone following them. About a hundred feet behind, the slim figure of a girl, wearing some sort of uniform, from a drive-in or theater, passed under a dim light that lit one of the warehouse doors.

Chris didn't like even a slip of a girl walking behind him in this neighborhood. He walked faster to leave her behind. But when he glanced back again, she was still there. He slowed to let her pass. She slowed her pace to match his and remained behind. Chris resumed his former pace and she followed him all the way home.

He went down the swaying gangplank to the houseboat and turned on the porch to try to get a good look at her as she passed. But she had gone through the dim light and was disappearing into the night. Just an accident, he told himself. He was getting jittery because this was a tough neighborhood.

The following night, the girl was behind him again. Then he knew the first night was no accident. He wondered if she was trying to steer him toward a couple of friends, waiting behind a lumber pile or around a building corner. He dismissed the idea. To do that she should be ahead of him. But maybe she was new at this. He thought of turning suddenly and confronting her. But that could be just what she and her friends wanted, a good excuse to jump him.

He kept walking, his eyes darting about in the dark for a club or something to use as a weapon. Then he remembered he had Mike. There could be no better weapon. He shortened up a little on the leash and said in a low voice, "Keep your eyes and ears open. We could have trouble any minute."

Chris paid no further attention to the girl behind him. At his own walkway, he hurried down and at the bottom turned quickly. The girl walked by without a glance his way. As she passed under the streetlight that lit the top of the walkway, Chris had a brief look at her. She was about his age, maybe a little younger. She had dark, shoulder-length hair that glistened in the light. She was wearing the uniform and now he was sure it was a drive-in restaurant outfit. Then she was gone.

The following night he asked Bruno about her, but the fat baker shook his head. "Don't fit anybody I know. You don't see many girls down here, especially at night."

The girl didn't appear that night or the next night. Chris caught himself looking for her and feeling vaguely disappointed when she didn't show. The third night, Mike swung his head around, ears erect. Chris looked, and there she was. Once again she seemed to be alone. She matched her walk to his and remained carefully behind.

Chris walked straight on until he came to a lumber pile that sat in the deep shadows of a building. He stepped quickly behind it, jerked Mike with him and waited. A moment later, the girl hurried by. He stepped out and grabbed her arm. She let out a frightened cry and tried to pull loose.

"You've been following me," Chris accused. "Why?"

42

She kept jerking and crying, "Let me go! Let me go!"

Chris shook her arm and said angrily, "Shut up and listen to me. I'm not going to hurt you. But this is the third night you've followed me. Now why?"

"I live down here. I was just going home. Let me go! Let me go!"

He shook her again. "You were following me. I can tell. I don't like anybody walking behind me down here. Not even a girl. Now, why? You'd better tell me."

"It's scary alone at night. You had this big dog, so I followed you. Nobody would bother you when you had the dog. I live two houseboats beyond you."

Chris let go her arm then and asked curiously, "How do you know I wouldn't jump you?"

"The dog," she said promptly. "Nobody with a dog like this would bother anyone."

Her reasoning didn't make much sense but Chris said, "Well, all right then. Come on. There's no sense you trailing along behind."

She walked beside him looking straight ahead. Mike trotted at the end of the leash leading the way. Finally she said, "I like your dog. I liked him the first time I saw him. What's his name?"

"Mike," Chris said.

Again they walked in silence. "Are you a relative of the Careys?"

"That's the people that own the houseboat where I live?"

"Yes."

"I never met them."

She asked next, "Are you going to stay?"

"Till they get back, I guess."

"That'll be almost a year."

"I know."

She didn't speak again until they were almost to Chris's walkway. Then she asked, "Are you a guard at the post office?"

"Yes," Chris said. "The dog give me away?"

"Nobody takes a big dog like that to work with them except for a good reason."

"You know more about me than I do you," Chris said. "I'd guess you're an usher in a theater or a carhop at some restaurant, by the uniform. I'll say carhop."

She smiled. She had a nice open smile. "Carhop," she said. "I live two houseboats beyond you, with my father. He's skipper of one of the harbor tugs that pushes ships around."

"Why does he let you take a job that makes you walk home alone, down here, this time of night? It's dangerous even for a man."

She didn't answer for a moment; then she said quietly, almost to herself, "I don't think he knows. He's never asked me and I haven't told him."

"I see," Chris said, but he didn't.

She explained, "My father practically lives aboard the tug. My mother used to say he was married to a tug. He only comes home about once a week, mostly for me to wash his clothes." There was a touch of anger in her voice. "Sometimes I don't see him more

44

than a few minutes a week. He wouldn't worry about me, no matter where I worked."

Chris had nothing to say to that, and they walked in silence. They began to pass moored houseboats and she said, "The second night I followed you there was someone else following you, too."

"I only saw you," Chris said.

"He walked in the shadows right up against the buildings."

"You're sure? Mike usually spots people either ahead or behind us."

"When Mike looked back, maybe he saw both of us. This man was behind me the first time."

"Maybe he was following you."

"I thought that the first time, so I stayed as close to you and Mike as I could. The next time I saw him, he was behind me again. When we got down along here, where it's darker, he must have had trouble keeping track of you. Even I couldn't see you too well. Anyway, alongside that big long warehouse back there, he had disappeared when I glanced back. The next thing I knew, he came out ahead of me at the other end of the warehouse. Oh, he was following you all right."

"Then what happened?"

"We were right close to your place when he suddenly stepped behind an old boat sitting on blocks on the dock, and that was the last I saw of him. Why would someone be following you?"

"I don't know," Chris said. "Did you see him again?"

"No."

"Probably was just curious."

They passed through the light over Chris's walkway, and a hundred feet farther on, the girl stopped at another lighted walkway. "This is where I live. Thanks a lot."

Chris leaned against the walkway railing. "How long have you been working nights?"

"I started the first night I followed you. I was working days but another girl had more seniority and bumped me· off the day job. I don't mind the night work. The tips are better. I just don't like walking the seawall alone."

"How do you get to the bay from uptown?"

"The bus brings me to the seawall."

"I'll wait for you from now on. If I don't meet you at the bus stop, I'll be at that big bakery a couple of blocks further on. I usually stop in for a cup of coffee before going home."

"I don't always get off the same time," she said. "Sometimes if it looks like a customer might leave a big tip, I stay until he leaves."

"I'm in no rush," Chris said. "I'll meet you at the bus stop or the bakery."

She patted Mike's head. "I don't want to be a bother."

"No bother. I don't like walking down here alone even with Mike along. Two makes it that much safer."

"All right," she said. "Thanks."

There was a commotion and much splashing below them. The two ducks Chris had seen before swam out of the shadows. The girl said, "Oh, there you are. I brought you something." She dug into her purse and brought out a napkin-wrapped package that held a piece of cake and parts of two sandwiches. She broke them into pieces and tossed them into the water. The ducks scrambled excitedly gobbling up every piece. She smiled down at them and said, "Andy and Angelina wait for me every night. I almost always bring them something."

"Andy and Angelina," Chris said. "Sure funny names."

"I guess so. But they're funny ducks. At first there was just Andy. Then Angelina came. They've been here almost two years now." The ducks finished their meal and swam off between the houseboats, talking amiably to themselves.

Chris said, "I don't know your name."

"Jennie Quinlan."

"Mine's Chris George." He watched her run sure-footedly down the swinging walkway, then he turned toward his own place.

Mike stopped so suddenly that Chris almost ran into him. His head was up, ears pricked forward. His whole body had that tense, ready-to-charge look. His attention was centered on an old boat, sitting on a pair of wooden horses on the dock, about a hundred feet away. Chris thought he glimpsed a shadow of movement there, but he wasn't sure. He debated going over and looking, then decided against it. He pulled on the leash and said, "Come on, Mike. Let's go."

They went down the swaying walkway to the houseboat. On the porch Chris turned quickly and looked toward the old boat. He saw nothing. But something had certainly caught Mike's attention.

The following night, Chris and Mike waited at the bus stop for Jennie so they'd be sure not to miss her. Mike's sharp eyes picked her up immediately. Jennie saw them and began to run. "Gee," she panted, "I'm glad you're here. I was afraid you might not be."

"I told you I'd wait," Chris said.

"I was just afraid you wouldn't." They walked along the seawall, Mike leading the way. Opposite the lighted bakery, Chris said, "How about a cup of coffee and a doughnut, or does feeding other people all evening turn you off food?"

"It should," she said, "but it doesn't."

The restaurant was empty of customers. They were sitting on stools at the counter, Mike between them, when Bruno came from the back room. Flour was dusted along his arms and across his fat face. He smiled and said to Chris, "You and Mike are in mighty nice company tonight."

Chris introduced Jennie, and Bruno's black brows jumped in surprise. "You any relation to Captain Quinlan, the skipper of one of the big harbor tugs?"

"My father," Jennie said.

"How about that!" Bruno's broad face wreathed in smiles. "The Captain stops in here most every week. He's crazy about cinnamon rolls and maple bars. But he's been holding out on me. He's never said one word about having a daughter. I'm going to have to get on him for that. Mighty closemouthed man, your dad."

"Yes, he is," Jennie said.

They had coffee and doughnuts. Bruno brought out broken pieces for Mike, then talked happily to Jennie all the time they were there. "Not many times a girl comes in here this time of night," Bruno explained. "You made my day."

When they were finally walking down the seawall again, Chris said, "Your boyfriend won't like me taking you home every night."

"No boyfriend," Jennie said.

"Oh." Chris found nothing to add to that.

Mike turned half sideways, his head swung back, ears erect.

Jennie glanced back immediately and said, "Don't look now, but the man I told you about is behind us again. I thought I saw him just before we went into the restaurant, but I wasn't sure. Now I am. Look back when I tell you to. He's across the street, walking in the deep shadow of that old warehouse. In a minute, he'll pass under a doorway light."

Chris was glad they had Mike along. He shortened up on the leash, bringing Mike closer to them.

Jennie asked, "Would Mike attack him?"

"I don't know. He hasn't been trained as an attack dog. But I think he might."

They went on, keeping the same pace. Jennie glanced back. "Pretty soon," she said. Then, "Now look! He's just coming into the light."

Chris swiveled his head. The man was passing directly under the light, walking close to the building wall. He was tall and slender. Chris got just a vague outline of features. He guessed the man to be in his thirties. But one quick look was all he needed. There was no mistaking the dark, well-pressed suit, the head up, shoulders back, chest out military carriage. He said, "You don't have to worry. It's someone from the Coast Guard. He's not interested in you. It's me he's watching."

"He's after you?"

"Not necessarily after me. He's just watching every move I make."

"But why?"

"Captain Wilson, and especially Lieutenant Ballard, are sure I know something about the whereabouts of two million dollars worth of heroin."

"Heroin! Two million dollars!" Jennie stopped dead and stared at him.

Chris took her arm. "Keep walking. Don't look back anymore." While they walked, Chris told her all about himself and Mike, how he'd come to own the dog, and why they now lived in the houseboat. "So you see," he finished, "Captain Wilson and Lieutenant Ballard have no love for me. Especially Ballard. I did give his program a black eye and he's not a forgiving man. I believe I know how he thinks," he said thoughtfully. "He doesn't have to watch me on the base or at the post office. No unauthorized person's allowed on either property after hours. But when I leave at midnight, I'm free. That's when he figures I might contact somebody. That's when he keeps tabs on every move I make."

"But you don't know anything—or do you?" Jennie asked.

"No more than you do, but they're not convinced of that."

"If you don't contact anyone in any way, they'll know you're not guilty, won't they?" Jennie reasoned.

"Maybe," Chris said. "I don't know. I may have to live with this as long as I'm in the Coast Guard."

"I think they'll get smart and know," Jennie said.

They passed his walkway and came to Jennie's. She said, "Don't wait for me tomorrow. It's my night off. It was nice knowing somebody was waiting for me." She ran down the walkway, stopped halfway, dug into her purse, and brought out the scraps she'd saved. Andy and Angelina glided out of the shadows and began scrambling and quacking loudly for the scraps she tossed them. Then she waved to Chris and went inside.

Chris waved back. Then he stood a moment smiling as the two ducks swam around the corner of the house, talking away and then disappearing.

He went on to his own houseboat. The coastguardsman had disappeared, or maybe he was somewhere in the dark watching. From now on, he could expect to be watched with suspicious eyes. The thought made him feel helpless and trapped.

4

Chris and Mike did not wait for Jennie the next night. When they stopped at the bakery for their nightly coffee and doughnuts, a single man sat on a stool at the counter. He was a husky, middle-aged man in a blue seaman's jacket and officer's cap. Even hunched over the counter eating the last of a cinnamon roll, he looked big. A faded seaman's bag was propped against the counter at his knee.

Chris took an end stool and Mike sat on his tail beside him, black nose twitching as he sucked in the tempting smells. The man glanced at him. He had a broad, scowling face and black eyes beneath the bushiest, most scowling brows Chris had ever seen. His skin was burned leathery brown.

Bruno came in from the back room, his fat face wreathed in smiles. "Chris," he greeted, "you're alone tonight. No girl friend?"

"Not tonight," Chris said.

Bruno looked at the seaman and said, "This's someone you ought to know, Chris. This is Captain Quinlan. Captain, this is the boy I've been telling you about."

So this was Jennie's father. His black eyes hit Chris like a physical blow. He swung around on the stool and faced Chris squarely. "Bruno tells me you're a sailor."

"Coast Guard," Chris said.

"Same thing." Captain Quinlan's voice was flat. "Keep away from my daughter, sailor. I won't have her hanging around with the likes of you."

"We're not 'hanging around' as you put it, captain," Chris explained. "She's afraid to walk home alone at midnight along the seawall. I walk with her, that's all."

"That's no excuse." Captain Quinlan was getting angry at being crossed. "There's nothing wrong with walking this seawall night or day. I've walked it for years. You keep away from Jennie."

"It's all right for a man," Chris pointed out. "It's not safe for a girl."

"Safer than walking alone with some two-bit sailor like you. I know you guys. Been watching your kind for years. I won't have her hanging around with any serviceman. Understand?"

Chris's own temper began to boil at the captain's unreasonableness. "Then maybe you'd better see that she gets home safe," he said recklessly. "That's all I'm doing. And I'll go on doing it, as long as she's afraid or until she tells me to stop."

Captain Quinlan moved with surprising suddenness for such a big man. He leaped off the stool and was on Chris in a bound. His big hand slashed across Chris's face with stunning force and rocked his head back.

"I'll teach you to talk back to me," he raged. He struck again, knocking Chris half off the stool. Captain Quinlan was drawing back to strike again when Chris ducked his head and plunged off the stool, headfirst into his middle. The force of his drive sent the big man stumbling back. He tripped over his seabag and sprawled on his back with Chris on top of him, smashing at his face with both fists.

Captain Quinlan was too strong. He rolled Chris off him, came on top, and began hammering at Chris.

Then Mike went into action. With a snarling roar, he landed on Captain Quinlan's back and sank his teeth into the upraised arm.

Captain Quinlan yelled in surprise. He heaved upright swinging his arm and shook Mike off. Mike landed six feet away and charged back to the attack, teeth bared, snarling horribly. Captain Quinlan grabbed the seabag and held it in front of himself like a shielf to fend off the raging dog. Mike attacked the bag. He got his teeth into it and the Captain tried to shake him loose. The bag ripped open. Dirty clothes flew in all directions. Mike lost his bite and went skidding across the floor. He was charging back to attack when Chris grabbed his collar and yelled, "Cut it out, Mike. Cut it out! Down! Down!" He clung to the collar and cuffed Mike's ears.

Captain Quinlan was rushing forward aiming a mighty kick at Mike when Bruno ran around the counter, grabbed him and wrestled him away. For a fat man, Bruno was surprisingly strong. He lifted Captain Quinlan of his feet and slammed him up against the counter. "Knock it off," he shouted angrily. "Knock it off. What's got into you anyway?"

For an instant Chris thought the angry Captain Quinlan would attack Bruno. Then, surprisingly, he calmed down. "All right," he panted. "All right." Without another word, he began gathering up his clothes and stuffing them into the bag. Bruno helped him. Only after he finished and tossed the seabag over his shoulder, did Captain Quinlan look at Chris, kneeling on the floor holding the still growling Mike.

He pointed a big finger at Chris and said ominously, "If that mutt ever looks at me again, I'll break every bone in his body. And you keep away from Jennie, or you'll get the same thing." With that he stalked out and slammed the door.

"Whew!" Bruno wiped his big face and went back behind the counter. "What the devil got into him? He had no call to jump you like that. You're doing him and his daughter a favor. I've known him about four years and he never went off the deep end like this before. Man, he really goes berserk. You all right?"

Chris rubbed his cheek that was beginning to swell and turn beet red and nodded. "He's sure got a hard hand."

"He's got that all right. Lucky for you Mike jumped

him, or you might have got quite a pounding before I could pull him off. I'd say Mike has earned a couple of extra bites of doughnut, wouldn't you?"

"I sure would," Chris said.

Bruno handed Chris a doughnut. He broke it up and Mike ate it, waving his tail happily. "You did just fine. I wasn't sure you'd tackle a man." He asked Bruno, "Did you tell Captain Quinlan that I was seeing Jennie home?"

"Sure I did." Bruno thought a moment. "I didn't say one thing bad about you. I bragged you up to beat the band. I thought he'd be pleased that somebody was looking out for his daughter when she makes this long walk at night. I would, if she was my girl. I sure didn't dream anything like this would happen." He shook his head. "I never seem to learn. Me and my big fat mouth almost got you beat up good. I sure am sorry."

Chris finished his coffee and stood up, fishing in his pocket for change. Bruno held up a hand. "Not to-night. This one's on the house."

Chris thanked him and was about to leave when Bruno asked, "You going to go on walking Jennie home?"

"Of course."

"Good. From now on, I keep my mouth shut. I don't know a thing." Bruno held up a hand as if taking an oath. "One thing, if you see the captain in here in the future, don't come in."

"I won't," Chris said.

The moment he stepped outside, Chris saw the man standing in the deep shadow of the building across the

56

street. He looked hard at him but there was nothing familiar about the vague shape. Of course he'd seen the fight with Captain Quinlan and would report it to Lieutenant Ballard. The lieutenant could be depended on to twist the incident any way he could to damage Chris. He was suddenly tempted to cross the street, to confront the man and accuse him of following him, and to demand an explanation.

But then he knew it would do no good. The man would be foolish to admit he was following Chris, and even if he did, it would gain Chris nothing. That fellow was simply following orders. Chris turned and walked off. Mike led the way, tail waving, sharp ears pricked forward. Chris glanced back several times before he reached his own walkway. He saw the man once; then he seemed to disappear. But Chris knew he was back there somewhere in the dark, watching every step he took.

Next morning Chris's mouth and the side of his face were swollen. It was hard to eat or smile. At the base they kidded him about forgetting to duck, or had he maybe walked into a door? Lieutenant Ballard came in, looked at him sharply, but said nothing.

Jennie was late. Chris waited for her at the bus stop. She looked closely at his face and said, "I'm sorry for what happened last night. My father has a temper. Does it hurt a lot?"

"I've been hurt worse," Chris said. Jennie kept her face turned partially away, and he asked, "What's wrong?"

"Nothing," she murmured.

He put a hand under her chin and pulled her face around. In the light from a near building, one eye looked discolored and her lips were swollen. Chris was shocked. "Your father did that to you, just because I walked home with you?"

"He has a temper," she repeated.

"That's an excuse?" Chris blurted.

"He doesn't need an excuse. You don't know my father."

"Tell me about him."

Jennie didn't answer for a moment. Then she said, "He tolerates me. I don't mean as much to him as Mike does to you."

"What about your mother?"

"They're divorced. Mother's married again. Her new husband didn't want me around, so father took me in."

"Took you in, or you came?" Chris asked shrewdly.

"Came, I guess. I had no place else to go."

"You must have other relatives."

"None that would be interested in me."

"You're old enough. You can leave, find an apartment and be on your own."

"I tried to leave once. He found me and brought me back."

"And slapped you around for leaving," Chris suggested.

"He has a temper," she said again.

They walked a little way in silence. Then Chris said, "It doesn't make sense. He doesn't want you around, or he acts that way. But he won't let you leave either."

"It makes sense when you know him. When I left it was like disobeying a command, or going contrary to his wishes or . . ." She searched for words.

"Or standing up to him," Chris suggested.

She nodded. "He always has to be the captain."

"And you're afraid of him."

"Yes, but it's more than that. I don't make a lot of money carhopping. I couldn't afford to pay much rent and buy clothes and food and things. Besides, it's not as easy for a girl to live alone as it is for a boy. When you get out of the service, what will you do, Chris? Or do you plan to stay in and make it a career?"

"I've got a little less than a year. Then I've been offered a good job in electronics. I plan to take it."

"You see," she said, "you and Mike can live anywhere. You'll probably get a very good salary." She looked at him curiously. "Where will you live, Chris? Have you got that all planned, too?"

"I thought I had," Chris said. He told her about the little farm he'd bought a year ago and how he planned to remodel the buildings. "I'm pretty handy with tools. Now I'm about to lose it because of delinquent taxes. Buying Mike took all my money."

Jennie said, "Maybe something will happen before the year is up."

"I'm still hoping it will," Chris said.

"I hope it works out," Jennie said, "but you see, you can plan that way. I can't."

They came opposite the bakery and Chris started to turn in. Jennie stopped. "I don't want to go in tonight.

I don't want what's his name, Bruno, to see me like this."

"Guess I won't stop either," Chris said. They walked on. A minute later Jennie asked, "How long is that man going to follow you?"

"The coastguardsman? I don't know. Why?"

"He's behind us again."

"That figures," Chris said. "Don't look back. Don't let him know you suspect him."

"He's got to stop sometime."

"Sure. When Lieutenant Ballard is convinced I'm not mixed up in the drug business. That could be a mighty long time," he said thoughtfully.

Two nights later, Jennie figured the swelling had gone down enough in her lips and the dark circles faded from around her eye, so she agreed to go into the bakery again.

They fell into an easy pattern of meeting at the bus stop, going into the bakery for coffee and doughnuts, and walking home. They were followed religiously every night by the coastguardsman.

One night Chris's hand was on the doorknob of the bakery when they both noticed the man sitting at the counter drinking coffee. They instantly recognized the broad shoulders, the seaman's jacket, and captain's cap. Chris saw Bruno standing at the far end of the counter, covertly shaking his head and making signs for them to leave. They turned quickly away and hurried to get home ahead of Captain Quinlan.

Chris left Jennie at her walkway and returned to his own houseboat. Mike and he stood at a darkened window and waited. About ten minutes later, Captain Quinlan strode past, seabag over his shoulder. Mike growled deep in his throat. "I know"—Chris patted his head—"I don't like him either."

Next night when he met Jennie, she said that her father had returned to his tug that evening when she went to work.

Bruno grinned when they came through the bakery door and said, "Last night was close. After you left, I talked like a Dutch uncle to hold him here, but ten minutes was all I could manage."

"That was fine," Chris said. "Thanks."

"I owed you that," Bruno said. "It was my fault to begin with. But you kids be careful. Don't antagonize the captain anymore. I don't want another ruckus in here."

They were careful. From past experience, Jennie knew just about the nights her father would come home. Those nights, they did not visit the bakery, and Chris stopped at his own walkway and let Jennie go on alone.

It was the day after one of those times, when Captain Quinlan had been home, that Chris ran into his first serious problem at the post office. They were making the last tour of the night. The main floor was quieter than it had been earlier. It was close to the end of the shift and everyone was tired. No one gave them more than a tired glance or raised a hand in recognition as they passed.

They went up and down the aisles of the first floor, Mike trotting a step ahead as usual, tail waving, brown eyes and black nose working. They walked outside to look around. Only one of the twenty doors was open. A truck was there with two men unloading. Far down at the end of the building, three young fellows stood just inside the truck gate talking. When they saw Mike and Chris start toward them, they sauntered outside the fence and disappeared in the night. Chris stood there a minute thinking about them. He decided they were nothing to worry about and returned inside.

The people on the second floor were like those on the first, waiting for this last hour to pass so they could go home. The third and fourth floors were dead quiet. They padded down the carpeted corridors, glancing through darkened windows and trying doors, and returned to the first floor.

They went up an outside aisle, heading for their own little office. A pie cart loaded with packages stood at the end of the aisle. Mike started to squeeze past. Suddenly he stopped. His head came up, his ears shot forward, and his black nose was tilted toward the top of the cart. Before Chris realized what was happening, Mike reared up, front paws on the top shelf of the cart, fastened his teeth into a cardboard package, and hauled it off onto the floor. He began shoving it along the floor with his nose, trying to get a grip on it with his teeth.

Chris lunged and jerked it away from him. Mike reared up against Chris's chest and reached for the package again. "Cut it out, Mike! Down! Down! What's got into you. You've seen plenty of packages before." He cuffed Mike's ears and finally the dog dropped back to the floor, but he kept looking up at the package and whining.

Chris looked at the package. It was only about six inches square and wrapped in brown wrapping paper. Automatically he glanced at the address: C. K. Marquand, General Delivery. There was no return. The letters were square and thick and heavy, as if made with a felt pen. It felt like sturdy cardboard. Mike had sunk his big teeth through the top. He'd have to put some tape over those holes and return it to the pie wagon immediately. He glanced about to see if anyone was watching them. No one was.

Chris carried the package into his little room and closed the door. There he inspected it again and turned it over to see if Mike's teeth had damaged the other side. It was dented, but it had not been punctured. He hoped the contents had not been damaged. He shook the box and listened for the rattle of broken glass or something.

A thin film of white powder trickled out the holes Mike's teeth had made. He shook a little into his palm and looked at it. It was as fine as talcum powder. Powdered sugar. Why would anyone send a package of powdered sugar through the mail? He wet a finger, touched it to the powder and tasted it. Then he just stood there, his face twisted out of shape, and shock rolled through him in waves. What he had just tasted was heroin.

5

Chris knew what he had tasted was heroin, but his mind refused to accept it. He tasted the white powder again to be absolutely sure. There was no mistake. During the months of training in the drug-bust program, they had all tasted it so they'd know what they were looking for. Mike pawed at him, whining and looking up at the package anxiously. Chris pushed him down and said, "Be quiet, Mike. I've got to think."

He tried to reason what he should do. Months of training told him to notify the Coast Guard immediately. But that would involve Lieutenant Ballard, which meant trouble for Chris. Ballard already believed he was in with the mob and had helped set up the pie incident aboard the ship. Now if Chris appeared with heroin on his person, the lieutenant would certainly come up with reasons to insist he was guilty.

He might even figure that Chris had somehow got in too deep with the gang, was frightened, and was running to the Coast Guard for protection. He thought of calling the local police, but they'd call the Coast Guard because the waterfront was their area. It would end up with Ballard and Captain Wilson, no matter what law enforcement organization he called. He had to get rid of this himself.

Mike kept pawing at him and whining. "You didn't help me any this time," Chris said. "We've got a real problem."

Chris looked about the room. There was no wash-basin or toilet he could flush it down. There was a small table with a single drawer. He pulled it out, not really expecting to find anything. It was empty. He thought of stashing it there and letting whoever found it try to figure out how it got there. But that would never do. If it was found anywhere in his area, he'd immediately be connected with it because, once again, the Coast Guard would be called in. The only other thing in the room besides a chair was a small waste-basket.

There was a washroom at the far end of the building. He stepped outside and looked the big sorting room over. He'd have to carry the package the full length of the building to reach the washroom. More than two hundred feet. He'd have to pass maybe a dozen or more people to get there.

Chris noticed the clock on the nearby wall. It was within fifteen minutes of quitting time. People were already beginning to drift toward the washroom to clean up. By the time he got there, a half dozen people could be in the room. The washroom was out. He could not wait until everyone left and then slip out, because the crew for the graveyard shift was already filtering in. If he hung around he'd draw attention because they'd wonder why he was still here. Lou West, the grave-yard watchman who took his place, would be coming in any minute. He had to carry this heroin out on his person and dispose of it, and he had to get it out of sight in a hurry.

Chris went back inside, closed the door, and looked around. The package was too big to fit into his pocket. The brown bag he'd brought his lunch in still lay on the table. He found another in the wastebasket. He ripped the package open, poured half the powder into each bag, folded the tops tight around the packages and put one in each pocket. The cardboard box, he carefully ripped into small strips and stuffed into his hip pockets. He had barely finished when the shift changed, the door opened and Lou West, the grave-yard man, came in. He grinned at Chris and patted Mike's head. "All quiet, huh?"

"All quiet." Chris snapped the leash on Mike and they left with the rest of the crowd.

By the time they had traveled the second block, they were alone and headed toward the bay. Just as soon as they reached the bay, Chris told himself, he'd toss both paper bags and the torn up carton into the water and he'd be through with it.

They were within a half block of the seawall, and

Chris was beginning to hurry, when Mike's head came up, his ears shot forward, and he turned halfway around. Chris looked where his head pointed, and there against a building's dark wall was the familiar, indistinct figure, his Coast Guard tail. He'd not have seen him if Mike hadn't given the alert. Chris was suddenly tense and suspicious.

What was he doing so far up from the waterfront and this close to the post office? Chris usually picked him up somewhere along the seawall on the walk home. Did he know something? Could this heroin in his pockets be a deliberate plant to somehow get him involved? Did he guess Chris had the heroin on him?

If so, the man would challenge him before he had a chance to get rid of it. There would be other coastguardsmen lurking near, waiting to rush in and help. He glanced about but saw no one. If they caught him with the stuff on him, he'd never be able to explain it anyway. The temptation to run was almost overpowering. But that would be a dead giveaway of guilt. Walk, he told himself sternly, make them come and get you.

He took a shorter leash on Mike, pulling the dog closer to him, and walked straight ahead. He made a block, was in the middle of the next. There was Jennie's bus stop and the black surface of the bay beyond. Chris stole a glance behind him. The man was gone, but Chris was sure he was somewhere near—watching, waiting for just the right moment. He didn't dare toss these packages into the bay. The moment he tried, men would be on him. He had to try to take these packages home with him. For the first time, a furious anger rose in him—a burning hatred for Lieutenant Ballard.

Holding Mike so close brought the dog within the scent range of the heroin in Chris's pocket. He began to rear and sniff at the pocket. Chris muttered, "Cut it out, Mike. Down! Down!" But Mike had been trained to search out the smell of heroin, and there it was. He continued to jump and nip at the pocket. If he kept this up, Chris was afraid the man behind him would become suspicious. He tried to yank Mike down and hold him down with the leash. Mike took this as an indication to play and kept jumping and snapping at his pocket.

"All right, come on," Chris said and started to trot as if playing with Mike. "You want some exercise, we'll run." Mike tried to run beside Chris and jump at the pocket too, but his actions only made him look frisky.

When they reached the bus stop, the bus was there and Jennie was just getting off. "You're a little early," Chris said.

"It was a slow night," Jennie explained. "There were more girls working than customers. There was no use staying longer."

They started walking along the seawall, and Jennie said, "What's Mike jumping around for?"

"Frisky," Chris said. "All he wants to do is play tonight." He yanked Mike down and cuffed his ears. "Now just cut it out." At the unexpected rebuke, Mike finally quieted down. Chris let out more slack in the leash, to get him further away from his pocket.

At the bakery, Chris tied Mike two seats from them; that, and the delicious bakery smells, kept him quiet.

They had their coffee and doughnuts, and Bruno brought out some broken pieces for Mike. As soon as they finished, Chris untied Mike's leash and prepared to leave.

"Hey," Bruno complained, "what's the rush? It's early yet."

"Early for you," Chris said, "late for me. I've got to get up for my shift at the base and I've had a tough evening."

"You call just walking around that post office work?" Bruno chided.

"It was tonight. A couple tried to swipe some packages off a truck," Chris lied. "Mike and I must have chased them half a mile trying to catch them."

"Did you?" Jennie asked.

Chris shook his head. "Those kids could run like deer."

Bruno lifted a fat hand. "See you tomorrow night."

Outside, away from the bakery smells and close to Chris again, Mike went back to trying to get at Chris's pocket. Chris finally slapped his ears again and said sharply, "Cut that out."

Jennie asked, "Is anything wrong?"

"No, why?"

"You seem sort of nervous." Then she added after a moment, "So does Mike."

"He's just got a streak of wanting to play. I just don't feel like it tonight."

Mike looked around about then, ears erect, head up.

"That man is behind us again," Jennie murmured. "Does his following us every night bother you?"

"Yes, it bothers me. But there's nothing I can do about it."

"He's been following us almost every night for two weeks. It seems he should get tired of it pretty soon or be convinced you have nothing to do with it."

"I've been hoping so," Chris said, "but Lieutenant Ballard is a very determined man, and Mike and I did give his drug-bust program a black eye. Lieutenant Ballard took it very personally, and he's not the kind to forgive and forget in a hurry. I'm hoping that Captain Wilson won't go for this much longer and will order Ballard to call off his tail."

At Jennie's walkway, Chris said good night to Jennie, and Mike and Chris returned to their own houseboat. He glanced about for the Coast Guard tail but didn't see him. But he knew that he was watching the houseboat from somewhere near.

His kitchen was on the bay side of the houseboat. No one could see into the room from onshore. Chris left the light on in the living room and hall, went into the dark kitchen and took the packets from his pockets, and emptied the contents into the sink and ran it down the drain. The empty paper bags and the torn up carton he shredded and burned in the sink. He washed the ashes down the drain, then carefully washed the sink with soap and a rag.

Later Chris lay in bed, Mike curled up at the foot, and looked out the window at the black, mysterious bay, thinking about the night's happening. While he had that heroin on his person, he'd been in a very delicate situation. If he'd been caught, then he'd be court-martialed for sure. That meant kicked out of the service with a dishonorable discharge. But even worse, the electrical firm he hoped to work for when he left would never hire him.

Lieutenant Ballard had said that six-ounce package they'd found aboard the freighter was worth about eighteen thousand dollars. He'd had about half a pound in his hands tonight. He had washed more than twenty-four thousand dollars' worth down the sink drain. That would have paid for the farm, new buildings and really set him up. There was a slight noise outside and Andy and Angelina glided past under the window making soft quacking sounds to themselves. "You've got no problems," he said to them. "You don't know how lucky you are."

Chris was anxious the following night as he and Mike passed up and down the aisles. He kept his eyes open for any brown cardboard package about eight inches square sitting on a shelf or pie wagon. Every time Mike passed one, he held his breath. He was amazed how many packages that shape and size there were. But they got through the whole evening and nothing happened.

They got through the next night the same way, and Chris began to relax. They had been to Bruno's, had their coffee and doughnuts, and were walking along the seawall when Jennie said, "Chris, that man that's

71

been following us—the Coast Guard tail— I haven't seen him. Have you?"

"No," Chris said. The truth was he'd been so preoccupied with thoughts of another heroin package that he hadn't even looked for the tail. "He's probably there all right. We just haven't looked close."

"I have," Jennie said. "And Mike hasn't once acted like there was anyone there."

"Maybe Mike's getting used to him just as we are."

"I've been looking," Jennie insisted. "Always before, I glimpsed him passing under a light or walking in the shadow of a building. I'd recognize his shape anywhere: tall, slender, walks very straight and takes quick steps."

"The military manner," Chris smiled. "Maybe they've changed men and a short, fat guy's doing it now."

"Be serious," Jennie said. "Fat or thin, I tell you I haven't seen anybody."

"He may be up ahead waiting someplace," Chris said. "But we'll keep an eye out for him. And Mike, you look sharp."

They went all the way to Jennie's walkway and saw no one. And Mike gave no indication that anyone else was about. Jennie said, "You told me they'd stop following you when this lieutenant at the Coast Guard was convinced you had nothing to do with the drugs. Does this mean he's convinced?"

Chris looked at Mike walking calmly straight ahead. He looked around at the surrounding dark and saw no one. "Maybe," he said, his voice full of doubt. "But don't count on it. I know Ballard."

The following night, Chris had his mind on the tail. He looked for him the moment he stepped outside the post office. He saw no one. He and Jennie did not see anyone on the walk home, and not once did Mike show signs that anyone was near.

"I'll bet I'm right," Jennie smiled at him. "They're through following you."

"You could be right," Chris agreed. "Yes, sir, you sure could." For the first time he felt a great weight had been lifted from his shoulders.

A minute later, Mike suddenly swiveled his head, his ears shot erect, and a low growl came from his throat. Chris looked back. Several hundred feet off, he made out the vague shape of a big man striding toward them. He was bent slightly forward under the weight of a bag over his shoulder. "Your father!" Chris said.

Jennie whispered, "Oh!" in a frightened voice and ran down the walkway and disappeared in the shadow of the porch.

Chris stepped quickly behind a huge empty box a few feet away and crouched down. He held Mike close and whispered, "Be quiet. Not a sound, hear?"

A minute later Captain Quinlan strode by and went down the walkway.

The following night while making their first round, Mike knocked another brown package off a shelf and began pushing it excitedly along the floor, trying to get a grip on it with his teeth. Chris ran to retrieve it. The moment he picked it up, he knew what he had. It was the same kind of cardboard box, bound with an excessive amount of strapping tape. The address was in the same black, square letters that had been on the first one. This, too, was addressed to general delivery. There was no return address.

Chris carried the box into his room and closed the door. His heart was hammering. He had trouble keeping his hands steady as he examined the box. Mike had not punched a hole in this one, but the dog kept rearing against him, whining and reaching for the box. Chris pushed him down and grumbled, "Quit being so smart. You got me in a jam the other night with one of these, and now you've got me in another. I ought to give you away or something." Then he patted the big head to reassure Mike.

Chris debated what to do. He was tempted to slip it back on the shelf and let it go through. If he did, he'd have nothing to worry about. He'd be absolutely in the clear. Then he thought of all the people who'd be hurt using this white powder and knew he couldn't. He had to get rid of this one too.

He began to plan how he could do it. It was early evening. The washroom should be empty of people, or nearly empty, at this time. Again, he used his own lunch sack, found another in the wastebasket, and put half in each bag. He put these in his coat pockets. He tore the box into tiny chunks and put them in his hip pockets. He left Mike in the room and strolled the length of the building to the washroom. Only one man was there, busily scrubbing a pair of greasy hands. Chris pretended to wash his hands. Then he combed his hair, while he covertly watched the man and waited for him to leave. Finally the man finished and left. Chris quickly stepped into one of the open booths, dumped the contents of both packages into the bowl and flushed it down. He tore up the sacks and stuffed the pieces along with those in his hip pockets almost to the bottom of a half-full trash can. Then he left.

For the rest of the night, Mike and Chris walked up and down the aisles, but the dog found nothing more. But Chris was now convinced that the mail was being used to get the heroin out to the dealers. He wondered how long it had been going on and how much had been distributed that way. Just the past few days, he had destroyed nearly fifty thousand dollars' worth. The only thing he could do, without implicating himself, was to destroy the packages whenever Mike found them. Maybe after these people had lost a few more such shipments, they'd decide that using the mail was too expensive and quit. Once he'd made that decision, he felt much better.

That night when he left the post office at midnight, he looked carefully for the coastguardsman who'd been tailing him. He saw no one. He met Jennie and they went to Bruno's bakery for their usual coffee and doughnuts. On the walk home they both kept a sharp lookout and Mike gave no indication that anyone was following. "I told you they'd quit," Jennie said happily.

"This proves they're convinced you're not involved, doesn't it?"

"Maybe. I hope so."

"What else can it be?"

"By now that Coast Guard tail can't help but know that I'm aware of him, and of course he's told Lieutenant Ballard. So they figure I'm being careful. What better way to throw me off guard than to take the tail off for a couple of days and hope that I'll think just what we are thinking. Then, I'll get careless and make contact with somebody in the racket. They'll be right there to nab me."

"You really think that's how it is?" Jennie asked.

"I don't know. It's possible. A couple of more days should tell."

The next night, Mike found another package. It was the same size and color as the others, the same weight, wrapped the same way, and it had the same black, block-square printing. Again, there was no return address. Chris disposed of it the same way he had the second, in the washroom.

Three days passed. The Coast Guard tail did not follow them home. Chris was sure then that the tail had been taken off. Mike uncovered no more packages of heroin. The dope shippers, Chris reasoned, had probably found another way to distribute their wares because the loss through the post office was too great. His two most dangerous problems were solved. Chris felt good.

That night when they reached Jennie's walkway,

Chris leaned against the railing and said, "Remember the place I told you about, that I bought and wanted to move out to when I left the service?"

"You mean the little farm you're going to lose because of the back taxes?"

"That's it. Mike and I are going out there Sunday, just to see it again. Why don't you come along? I'll rent a car for the day."

Jennie hesitated. "I'd like to see it. But I don't know. It's getting about time for my father to come home again."

"If he comes home, we can put it off till another time. You can phone me."

"All right." Jennie smiled. "I'll fix up a lunch and we'll make it a regular picnic."

"Great!" Chris said. "If your father's not home, I'll get the car and be here about eleven o'clock."

Later Chris lay in bed and looked out the window at the distant lights of the city. He felt better than he had in years. The Coast Guard had called off its tail, the dope people had stopped using the post office, and Jennie was going out to the farm with him. Somewhere in the silence he heard Angelina and Andy quacking. You're not the only ones who've got it good, he thought.

6

That same evening, a meeting was held in a room in a small out-of-the-way motel. There were a dozen men present. They sat about on chairs, the bed, the davenport. A barrel-chested man, with a knife scar that angled down his cheek from temple to chin, sat in the only overstuffed chair. The way the rest looked at him and waited for him to speak, it was obvious he was the most important man in the room.

The scar-faced man took his time looking at each man in the room. Finally he said, "All right, we all know why we're here." His voice was harsh, as if his larynx had been damaged. "Three packages of merchandise have disappeared from the post office in the past few days." He pointed a big finger at three of the men. "Yours and yours and yours. That right?"

All three nodded and a thin, ratty-looking man said,

"Absolutely right. I've been practically out of business for a week. I go down to the post office to the general delivery window and call for my package like I've been doing for three years now. But nothing's there."

The scar-faced man looked at the two others, who both nodded. "That's right," one said. "That's just how it is. I go down there every day for a week and ask, figuring that maybe it's been overlooked or something. There's nothing. The street dealers are getting on me for more, and I'm about out. Something's got to be done in a hurry or I'm out of business, and so are they."

"We'll all be out of business," the scar-faced man said. "That's why I called you all here, to explain what's happened and what we're doing about it. It's better to meet this way than to hunt you up individually or to phone. Phones can be tapped. Now then, we've lost three deliveries in a row, almost one and a half pounds. A lot of money. It's got to stop. We've been using the post office for a drop and pickup for three years, and it's worked perfect until lately. We mailed it, you called and picked it up general delivery. Nobody was wise. No problems. Now somebody knows. We've got a problem."

"Maybe it was an accident and won't happen again," someone suggested.

The scar-faced man shook his head. "Once could be an accident. Twice, maybe. Three times in a row, never. We began checking to find out what happened. We put the stuff into the post office. It never went out.

Somewhere in the central post office those packages disappeared. That meant somebody had found them. Then we began checking out the people working there. It wasn't hard to pin down."

"The night watchman on the four-to-twelve shift retired recently. They hired a young kid about twenty to take his place. He's got one of those dope-sniffing dogs. It's the same kid and dog that was on their drugbust program and messed up that assignment on the freighter, *Coral Queen*, when the dog went for the pie. The dog found those three packages and the kid got rid of them."

"You're sure it was the dog found them?" someone asked.

"Positive. There's no way a workman could spot one of those packages among the thousands that go through every day. Nothing happened until that dog began sniffing around."

"How many people know?"

"Only the kid."

"How can you be sure?"

"If he'd said anything, the Coast Guard and local police would have heard. The place would be swarming with Coast Guard personnel and city detectives. And there's nobody around."

"Do we start sending it out to the dealers by runners?" someone asked.

"No runners," the scar-faced man said. "It's too easy for something to happen, an accident, a cop gets suspicious. The post office is perfect."

"Then we get rid of the kid and the dog."

"Just the dog. Without the dog, the kid's nothing."

"They can bring in another dog."

"Not in this case. That's where we're lucky. This kid's in bad with the Coast Guard now, and he's scared." The scar-faced man gave them Chris and Mike's history. Chris would have been amazed at what he knew. "I've got men coming tomorrow to take care of the dog. It may take a few days. Then we go back to operating just like before. There'll be a change in packaging, which I'll let you know about later. So everybody just sit tight till this is over."

No one said anything. They all knew this man. He came right from the top. The meeting was over. They filed out, got in their cars, and drove away.

Next morning, two men who had flown several thousand miles knocked on the motel door and were admitted by the scar-faced man. They sat on straight-backed chairs, held their hats in their hands, and listened while he sat in the overstuffed chair and talked. One of the men was tall and slender. He wore glasses and kept pushing them up on his nose with a nervous gesture as if they were loose. The other was very blond and stout. His eyes were such a pale blue that they seemed to have no color at all.

The scar-faced man said, "We brought you out here because for this job we want somebody that won't be known locally. As soon as you're through, you get paid and you leave. You understand about this job?"

"What's to understand," the blond man said. "You want somebody taken care of. We take care of him."

"Not somebody," the scar-faced man said. "A dog."

The two men exchanged looks. The one with the glasses said, "Let me get this straight; we came out here just to kill a dog?" He sounded insulted.

"A very special dog."

"A lousy mutt!" The thin one pushed his glasses up with an angry gesture. "They sent us clear out here for that?" He looked at the blond man. "How do you like that." Then he said to the scar-faced man, "For your information, we don't take care of mutts, no matter whose they are. Let the pound do it." He motioned to the blond. "Let's go. We've made a trip for nothing." He shook his head and rose. "A dog! A lousy dog!"

The scar-faced man let them get almost to the door; then he said quietly, "This just happens to be about the most special job you've ever been called on to do; otherwise it wouldn't pay ten thousand dollars."

The two men exchanged looks; then they returned to their chairs and sat down. "We're listening," the man with the glasses said.

"I said this dog was special. He's more special than any man. This so-called mutt has already cost us almost a hundred thousand dollars, and unless something's done about him in a hurry, he can ruin this whole drug setup here. This is the situation." The scar-faced man went into great detail about Chris and Mike. Who they were, what they were doing at the post office, how they happened to be hired, the pie incident aboard the freighter. He even told them about Chris's uncle and aunt and about his buying the old farm.

The thin man pushed his glasses up on his nose and smiled. "That sounds a little more like it. I can see you've got a problem, but not too complicated a one. It's still just a dog. We shoot him and that's the end of your troubles. The police, nobody, is going to make much fuss over just a dog."

"They will this one," the scar-faced man said. "He's a dope sniffer and everybody knows it. Unless this job's done very carefully, the Coast Guard and every law enforcement agency in this area will become suspicious and begin looking. If it called for just killing a dog, anybody could do that. The fact that we sent for you two and flew you all the way out here, ought to tell you something about how important this job is. This dog has to be gotten rid of in such a manner that nobody, but nobody, can connect it in any way with the post office. I want that understood right now. We've been using that post office for three years and it's been perfect. We intend to go on using it.

"If you can make it look like an accident of some kind, so much the better; like running him down with a car or drowning him, or even poisoning him, it'll draw no more than casual attention. Dogs are run down or poisoned or drowned every day. You can use a gun if you like. Just remember it has to be done far enough away so it doesn't draw attention to the post office. And then you've got to get rid of the dog so there'll be no evidence to show how he was killed."

"We can get rid of the dog so there won't even be a hair left around to show what happened to him," the blond man said. "But what about the kid? He'll know what happened to his mutt, no matter how careful we are. He can yell his head off."

"Sure he can yell, but who'd believe him? I'm betting he won't even peep. If he does, he implicates himself. He'd have to admit he found some drugs and then got rid of them without ever reporting it. There's a Coast Guard lieutenant who'd like nothing better than to nail this kid good. No, you don't have to worry about the kid. He's got himself into a corner. He has to walk mighty careful and keep his mouth shut. Just take your own time. Do it any way you like, but be dead sure you get rid of that animal, in a way no finger of suspicion can point toward us and the post office. When you've finished, come back here. Your money will be waiting. Then get out of town immediately."

The two men rose. The blond one said, "We'll take care of it. Your dog's as good as dead."

"That's how it has to be," the scar-faced man said.

7

Chris was still feeling good the next night when he got off shift and Mike and he headed toward Jennie's bus stop. Automatically he glanced about for the Coast Guard tail. But he saw no one. And to make matters even better tonight, Mike had found no square, brown box. Chris had the leash wrapped around his hand, and Mike trotted about eight feet ahead of him, looking about importantly.

Practically all the postal workers disappeared into cars, and by the time they had gone a block, they walked the dark alone. This time of night the street was usually empty of cars, and it was tonight, except for a coupe sitting in the shadows of the darkest part of the street.

They passed the coupe and Chris noticed the black bulk of someone inside. Mike turned his head and picked up his ears. Then they were past. Across the street and another block down was Jennie's bus stop. The bus swung out of a side street and stopped. In the light of the bus stop, Chris saw Jennie get off.

He stepped off the curb and began to hurry. They were halfway across the street, Mike pulling ahead the full length of the leash. Chris was smiling in anticipation of meeting Jennie. A car motor started off to his left and back up the block. The motor accelerated to a roar. There was the tortured squeal of tires. Some fool squirreling! The roar hit him like an advancing wave. He glanced to his left. Lights out, the parked coupe he had just passed was hurtling toward him like a black thunderbolt.

Chris acted without thinking. He let out a yell, "Mike back!" and the same moment yanked on the leash with all his strength and fell backward. Mike, expecting nothing, was suddenly jerked back a good yard. It was just enough so that the speeding car missed him, but so close it snapped the end of his tail.

The car went careening through the night to the first cross street. It turned there, the lights still out, and disappeared behind the wall of a darkened warehouse.

Chris scrambled to his feet. Mike was already standing, sharp ears shot forward, all attention as he looked off into the dark toward the fading sound of the roaring motor. Chris patted his big head and muttered, "That was close! Awful close! I'm sure glad you're all right."

Jennie came running up the block crying, "Chris, you all right? You all right?"

"I'm okay," Chris said. "He missed us."

"I saw it." Jennie was panting. Her eyes were big. "When you fell, I thought he'd hit you."

"Some fool drunk," Chris said. "Did you get a good look at the car?"

Jennie shook her head. "It happened so quick. All I saw was that it was dark and a coupe of some kind. I got a glimpse of a driver's head and shoulders, but that's all."

"That's about all I saw," Chris said. Then he remembered one other thing, a pair of tiny silvery flashes as the coupe roared by.

When they walked into the bakery a few minutes later, Bruno looked up and said, "What happened? You see a ghost or something?"

"Somebody almost made me one," Chris answered.

"A car almost ran him and Mike down," Jennie said. "I saw it."

Bruno shoved a cup of coffee in front of Chris and said, "You need this, friend. Drink up. Did you get a good look at the driver?"

Chris took a swallow of coffee and said, "Just a glimpse. It happened too fast and it was too dark and the car lights were out. I had the feeling there were two men in the car, but I'm not sure."

"Probably never see them again." Bruno drew a cup of coffee for Jennie. "Drink up and forget it." He brought out doughnuts. Chris ate his. Jennie was too upset and fed hers to Mike.

On the walk home, Chris was quiet, thinking about the car that had so nearly run them down. There was something strange about the whole incident, but he could not put a finger on it.

Jennie finally asked, "Are you still thinking about that car?"

"No," Chris lied. "I was thinking about going out to see my farm again tomorrow and the good time we can have. I've never shown it to anyone before."

"I'm going to pack a lunch." Jennie smiled up at him. "It'll be the first time I've ever gone out on a real picnic."

"Be my first time too," Chris said.

At Jennie's walkway, Chris said, "I'll pick up the car tomorrow morning and be here about eleven."

"I'll be ready," Jennie said.

Chris watched her run lightly down the walkway, disdaining the cables; then he turned back to his own houseboat.

The black bulk of a car sat far down the dock with its lights out. It hadn't been there when they passed. Or maybe it had. It was at the edge of the dock and beside an old pile of lumber. Both he and Jennie could have missed it. At this distance and in the dark, its shape resembled a little that of the one that had almost run them down. Mike was standing head up, ears erect, whole body alert. But that didn't mean anything. There was no one in sight. His sensitive nostrils could have picked up some wayward scent that interested him. Cut it out, he told himself sternly. That car is none of your business. You're getting jittery. He went down his own walkway. Andy and Angelina cruised out of the dark close beneath him, uttering companionable quacks. He grinned down at them and said, "And the same to you, too."

Next morning at eight, Chris and Mike headed out to rent a car. At the top of the walkway Mike stopped, nose down, sniffing. Chris said sharply, "Mike, cut it out." Mike had been trained not to eat anything unless it was expressly given to him. Chris looked at what he'd been nosing. Inch-square chunks of meat were lying about. Somebody's package had broken and they'd lost their stew meat. Chris kicked the chunks off the dock into the bay. There was a racket and excited splashing below. He looked over the edge of the dock. Andy and Angelina were rushing about, diving for the pieces of meat. Chris smiled and went on down the dock.

At ten-thirty he was back in front of Jennie's walkway in the rented car. Jennie came running up the walkway carrying a pair of paper bags and a big thermos bottle. Chris headed out of the city, Mike held down the back seat, big head resting on the back of the front seat between them while he watched the road ahead.

It was only seventeen miles from the city, down a narrow two-lane country road. The place looked just the same as it had when Chris was last here, six months before. The lawn needed mowing. The house and outbuildings needed paint, but Chris knew they were all sound. Chris turned Mike loose and the big dog dashed about inspecting all the buildings until

Chris ordered him to stay close. They walked about and Chris pointed out the different buildings, the barn, chicken house, tractor shed, well house. All the desire to live here and the pride of ownership welled up in him again, as it always did when he came out here.

"I used to walk by the place every day on the way to school," he explained. "Mr. Miller couldn't do much. He couldn't handle the tractor very well because he only had one good arm. I did his tractor work for him. It's real good soil. It only takes about thirty minutes to drive to that electrical plant, where I figure to work when I get out of the service." He wanted Jennie to be impressed, to like it and see all its possibilities, just as he did.

"I know it doesn't look so good now," he explained anxiously. "No place does when it's vacant, and the buildings are a little run down. But give me a week painting and cleaning up around here, and you won't know it's the same farm. Paint the outbuildings red with white trim, the house pure white," he said enthusiastically. "You'd never recognize it."

Chris unlocked the front door and they went inside. "The house can be remodeled. It's well built," he explained. "I can do that in my spare time. I'm pretty handy with tools." The house was completely barren of furniture. "The Millers took everything with them. Furniture would make a world of difference."

There were five rooms, and they wandered from one to another. Mike padded ahead of them, nosing into corners and behind doors as he'd been trained to do when searching for drugs.

Jennie didn't say anything, but her brown eyes were as busy as Mike's nose. She looked out the windows, rubbed a finger along the dusty sills, peeked into empty closets and drawers. In the kitchen she turned on the faucets, but no water came.

"Electricity's turned off," Chris explained, "so the pump doesn't work. There's a good well; more than a hundred feet deep."

"Oh," Jennie said.

They returned to the front door and Chris asked, "Well, this is it. How do you like it?"

Jennie smiled then. "It looks awfully good to me. I've lived almost my whole life on a houseboat. I've always dreamed of living on something like this, a farm. How many acres did you say you had?"

"Ten, it's not big."

"It is to me," Jennie said.

"A family could live on it just fine," Chris said. "Keep a cow or two, a couple of hundred chickens, grow all your own meat and vegetables. And there's a creek on the place, too. Right down there"—he pointed—"where those trees are. It's a year-round creek. It even has fish in it."

"Let's have our picnic there."

Chris got the two paper sacks of sandwiches and the thermos bottle, and they hiked off across the open pasture to the trees. Mike raced ahead, tail waving happily as he investigated every bush and grass clump.

The creek was a clear, small stream about eight feet wide that wandered between low banks through the trees. They sat on the bank and Jennie opened the sacks and took out the sandwiches and paper cups. They ate, watching the water and Mike, who was enjoying himself, sniffing along the bank and investigating a frog he'd found.

Jennie said, "You told me you were going to lose it. Are you sure?"

"It looks like I'm going to," Chris said. "The way things have turned out lately, I don't see how I can raise the money to pay the Millers the thousand I owe them every year, plus the delinquent taxes. I keep hoping something will happen and I can get the money, but nothing has."

"How much back taxes did the Millers owe?" Jennie asked.

"Right up to the last year. I'm not even sure they knew that. But it comes to a little more than fifteen hundred dollars."

Jennie said, "I watched you back there showing me through the house. You really love it, don't you?"

Chris nodded. "My folks died in a house fire when I was ten, and I came to live with an uncle and aunt. But they never let me feel I belonged, or that anything was mine." He looked around. "This made me feel like I could put down roots, that I was somebody."

Jennie said thoughtfully, "It would be a shame to lose it. Somehow you've got to keep it, Chris."

Chris shook his head. "I don't see any way. None at all."

Jennie asked, "Suppose you just had to raise the thousand dollars to pay the Millers. Could you do that?"

"I could just about make that," Chris said. "In fact, if I could somehow make the taxes too, this year, from then on it'd be clear sailing. I've only got eight months to go on my enlistment; then I've got a good job waiting for me that'll pay three times as much as I make now. Once I get on that job, keeping the farm going will be a cinch."

Jennie sat staring at the water. Then she said quietly, "I'll pay the taxes."

"You!" Chris was shocked. "I didn't mean . . ."

"I want to do it. It's not right that you should lose a place that means so much to you. I've only been working a couple of months, but I've already saved over three hundred dollars."

Chris kept shaking his head, and when she finished he said, "Thanks. Thanks a lot. But you can't. Your father would never stand for it."

"He won't know," Jennie said. "He doesn't pay any attention to what I do with my money, or to me either," she said bitterly. "He mostly keeps me around to look after the house when he's not there and to wash his clothes when he comes home about once a week."

"I don't know how soon I could pay you back," Chris said. "I guess you'd have to be a partner in this place."

Jennie looked around, smiling. "Part owner in a farm," she said, "a home. I'd like that."

Chris had forgotten his sandwich, forgotten Mike wading excitedly belly-deep in the creek, chasing the frog. Something wonderful was happening to him. Then he knew it had been happening for weeks—on those walks home at night along the seawall—drinking coffee and eating doughnuts at Bruno's—standing at the bus stop waiting for Jennie to get off—and the good talks they had. They'd all been drawing them closer together. He found himself suddenly saying, "We can fix it up, Jennie, do it all ourselves. It'd be a great place for us to live."

"Us! You mean us!" Jennie's eyes were big and very brown.

His tongue had tripped him up, or maybe he'd been thinking this for some time and now was the first chance the thought had to come out. He rushed on. "Why not, Jennie? I've got no folks at all, and the way your father treats you, you might as well not have. Everybody's got to have somebody and feel like they belong someplace. We can have each other and belong here. Why not, Jennie?" he repeated.

Jennie looked at the ground and pulled a grass stem and broke it in two. The creek gurgled softly at their feet. Downstream a little way, Mike barked sharply at the disappearing frog. "We haven't known each other very long," she said.

"It doesn't take days to make it long," Chris said. "It seems like I've known you all my life."

"Seems that way to me, too," Jennie said. "Lots of fellows stop by the drive-in. Some I've known a lot longer than I have you, but I don't feel this way about any of them." She looked directly at Chris then and asked, "Is this how it happens, Chris?"

"I don't know. I guess with us it is."

"I've got to think about it some more."

"How long?" Chris asked.

She smiled mischievously. "About as long as it takes to eat this sandwich."

That was when they heard the sound of the shot and Mike's surprised yelp.

Chris jerked his head toward the dog just in time to see him bounce into the air and a spout of water explode under his startled nose. A second shot went over his head and the bullet dug into the far bank. A third followed almost immediately and plowed into the water a foot ahead of Mike.

Some crazy city fool who hadn't the faintest idea how to handle a gun. Chris jumped up and started to yell at the top of his lungs. What he saw stopped the yell dead in his throat.

Two men were racing across the pasture toward them. They were carrying pistols. One was slender and wore glasses. The sun glistened on the lenses. The other was blond and heavyset. They ran with purpose, as if they knew exactly where they were going and what they were doing. Chris guessed instantly they were intent on reaching the creek and using those guns again. Danger yelled through him. He called to Mike, "Here! Here! Mike! Come here!" He grabbed Jennie's hand and jerked her to her feet. "Run," he commanded, "come on, run!"

Luckily Chris knew the area, having walked over it many times in past years. Just ahead, the bank rose to about six feet. They would be hidden until the men reached the creek. Chris's thoughts leaped ahead as they ran. Later he was surprised how clear his thinking was. That tough Coast Guard training paid off.

Up ahead, the creek made a sharp turn around a big rock onshore. There the water was about three feet deep and swift. A shallow wash cut into the creek bank coming down from the pasture. Jennie could not outrun the two men. Beyond the rock they'd be in plain sight of those men and their guns. At the rock he had to do something to slow them down.

The moment they came to the boulder, he jerked Jennie behind it and crouched down. The ravine was there. He pointed to it and said, "See that? Run up it. It'll bring you out in the pasture and you can see the house and the car. Get to the car as fast as you can and wait for me." He pressed the key into her hand. "Can you start the motor?"

"Of course."

"Start it. Take Mike with you and have the car door open for me."

"What're you going to do?" Jennie asked fearfully.

"I've got to slow up those two men if we're going to get away."

"No," she said, "I'm staying too."

"Do as I tell you! Quick! Take Mike with you. Go on! Run!" He shoved the big dog toward her, "Go with her, Mike. Go! Go!"

Jennie said, "Come on, Mike. Come!" They disappeared up the wash together.

Chris looked about for some kind of weapon. A few feet off lay a dead limb some six or eight feet long. He grabbed it and waited.

Chris heard them slipping and sliding over the wet rocks of the creek bank, then their tortured panting. He gripped the club and waited. They would be concentrating on keeping their footing, not looking for him. Chris drew a careful breath and brought the club back over his shoulder.

They stumbled around the corner of the rock, actually walking in the water close to shore and watching where they put their feet. They were walking practically side by side. Chris swung at their legs with all his might, hoping to knock them both off their feet.

The last instant, the one wearing glasses sensed his presence and glanced up. He opened his mouth to yell and throw himself out of the way. Then the club landed with a solid crack just below his knees and cut his legs from under him. He went over backward in the creek and began splashing frantically trying to regain his feet. The blond, husky man had not been touched. Chris swung up the club again. This one tried to duck the swishing club, lost his balance and fell. The club caught him in the stomach as he went down. The swift current rolled him over and over as he tried to gain his feet.

Chris dropped the club and sprinted up the wash.

A blue Ford coupe was pulled into the yard behind their car. Jennie had their door open for him and was looking back toward the wash. Mike was in the back seat. Chris jumped into the car. The motor was running. He backed around to circle the other car to go out to the road. Suddenly he stopped, jumped out and ran to the coupe. It took less than five seconds to snap up the hood, grab a handful of distributor wires, yank them out and throw them off into the deep grass and jump back into the car.

They were roaring out of the yard when the two men, guns in hand and soaking wet, stumbled out of the ravine. They stood there and watched as Chris roared off down the road. They made no effort to shoot.

After a mile or so, Chris eased up on the accelerator. There was no need to worry about those two following them. It was going to take most of the day to replace those wires he'd torn out of their car.

Jennie's eyes were still big and frightened, her cheeks flushed. She asked, "What was that all about, Chris? Who were those men?"

Chris shook his head. "I don't know who they are or what it was all about. I thought at first they were a couple of fools with guns. But they're not. They knew what they were doing. They meant business."

"What kind of business is shooting at people?" Jennie was getting over her fright and was becoming indignant.

"It makes no sense," Chris said. "But they were after us."

Jennie was thoughtful a minute; then she said, "Maybe they thought we were somebody else."

"Maybe," Chris said. But that explanation didn't satisfy him. Something kept nagging at him but he couldn't put a finger on it. The first couple of shots had come awfully close to Mike. But why would they be shooting at a dog, and if they were, why had they chased Chris and Jennie? They had certainly seen them.

They both lapsed into silence and drove the rest of the way to Jennie's houseboat. Mike was the only one not worried. He sat on the back seat, tongue run out in a dog grin, and looked out the window.

They rattled down the old dock, stopped at Jennie's walkway and got out of the car. Mike trotted to the edge of the dock and began to bark excitedly. They went to look.

Ten feet below, Andy and Angelina floated, wings spread open, their heads hanging straight down under the water. Chris ran down the walkway, grabbed an oar leaning against the porch rail and pulled them close where he could reach them. He laid them side by side on the porch. They were dead.

Jennie knelt beside him and stroked them and began to cry. "Poor Andy," she sobbed. "Poor Angelina." She looked at Chris, tears running down her cheeks. "I saw them early this morning and they were all right. What happened to them, Chris? What happened?"

Chris looked at the two dead ducks, but his thoughts were racing. Then, surprisingly, everything fell into place like the pieces of a puzzle. The dark car that had almost run them down last night, but missing him and almost getting Mike. Then the thing that had nagged at him today and last night. The quick, silvery flash as the car sped past last night, he'd seen again just an hour ago. Sunlight on the lens of a pair of glasses. Last night it had been the brief reflection of a distant streetlight. The car he'd seen parked down the dock last night. The small squares of meat he'd found on his walkway this morning and had kicked off into the bay. Andy and Angelina had been right there gobbling them up. Poison, poison meant for Mike. The rundown last night meant to get Mike. Not him. Those shots at the ranch hadn't even come close to Jenny and him. They had come close to Mike. They had been meant for Mike. Those two men looking very businesslike with their guns. He said in a shocked voice, "It's Mike they're after! They're trying to kill Mike! There's a contract out on Mike!"

8

Jennie's eyes were round and big with shock. "A contract!" she said, "You mean a contract like—like gangsters use to kill people?"

"That's right," Chris said.

"But that's crazy! Mike's a dog. Why would anybody want to kill Mike. Why would they go to all the bother to follow us way out in the country just to shoot a dog. Oh, no, you're wrong, Chris."

Chris shook his head. "I don't think so. Let's go inside. I'll tell you all about it."

Jennie sat in a chair in the living room, and Mike wandered about inspecting every nook with his nose while Chris explained how he'd found the heroin in the post office and destroyed it. He told her how the car had not tried to run over him last night but had tried to hit Mike. And he told her about the dark car that had been parked up the dock from his houseboat, and the chunks of meat he'd found on the walkway next morning and had kicked off into the bay. It was those chunks of meat that had killed Andy and Angelina. They were poisoned meat and had been meant for Mike. "There's no reason in the world for anyone to accidentally drop that meat there." And for a clincher he added, "Those shots out at the farm didn't come anywhere near us. They were all aimed at Mike. It's Mike they're out to get rid of."

"But putting out a contract to kill a dog doesn't make sense. Mike can't do anything to them," Jennie insisted.

"He can find the stuff. I can't."

"But Mike can't notify the authorities. You can."

"That's just it," Chris said. "I can't. I don't dare."

"Why not? The police would be very happy to know about it, I'm sure."

"If I notified the police," Chris explained, "they'd immediately get in touch with the Coast Guard because they're responsible for the waterfront and have their own drug-bust program. That would bring Lieutenant Ballard down on my back again."

"He should be very happy. You'd be giving him a, what do they call it, a lead, wouldn't you?"

"Sure. But if I walked in and said that I'd discovered that heroin was being shipped out through the post office, I'd have to tell them how I knew; then I'd have to admit I'd been destroying it, destroying evidence. Ballard already believes I'm in with the Mob. That's why he had the tail on me for nights. If I told him this story, he'd be sure of it."

"I still don't see how. Are you sure you're not borrowing trouble? Wouldn't telling him be proof of your innocence?"

"I know Ballard pretty well. He'd immediately jump to the conclusion that somehow I'd got in trouble with the gang. And if I was one of them, and had been destroying dope, believe me I *would* be in trouble with them. He'd think that as a last resort I'd run to the Coast Guard for protection. I'd be playing right into Ballard's hands. He'd crucify me."

"That doesn't leave you much choice except to run away," Jennie said.

"I've thought of it," Chris said. "But that's desertion. I'd have to change my name. I'd be running the rest of my life always looking over my shoulder. And I'd lose everything I've been working and planning for. Maybe it doesn't seem like too much. But it's awfully important to me."

"I know," Jennie said quietly. "I need a life like that as bad as you do."

"You mean, you're still willing to go through with it, like you said back there at the creek?"

"Well, of course. We're going to go ahead just—just like we planned. But how are you going to get out of this? You say you can't go to the police and you can't go to the Coast Guard. Then what can you do?"

Chris took a nervous turn about the room. "So far I've got Lieutenant Ballard off my back. He's no longer keeping tabs on me. That's one thing."

"He's not your problem. The two men back at the farm are. And they had guns. What about them?"

Chris shook his head. "Mike and those men." He looked down at Mike, who decided to curl up on the rug for a nap. "Not even those men," Chris said. "Mike's my whole problem. Those men know that without Mike I can't do a thing. He finds the stuff, I don't. Those men aren't bothering me. It's Mike they want. If I just had some friends clear out of the country I could send Mike to until this blows over. But I haven't."

"Maybe you could board him someplace for a couple of weeks," Jennie said hopefully.

"A couple of weeks wouldn't do it. When he got back he'd start right over again if I still worked at the post office. And I've got to keep that job. Besides, if I appeared at the post office without him, those men would guess what I'd done and start looking for him. All they'd have to do is check all the kennels. He'd be easy to find, and there he'd be easy to kill."

"You think those men will be watching you that close?"

"You can bet on it," Chris said. "And there's another thing; the post office hired me partly because I had Mike. Maybe they wouldn't want me without him. I sure have got myself, and Mike too, in a mess."

"You did what you had to, to keep Mike."

"I guess that's what I'll have to go on doing."

"How do you mean?"

"Keep avoiding them every way I can, so they won't get another chance to kill Mike."

"How will you do that?"

"Take different routes home. Keep my eyes open for them."

"That's not very much," Jennie pointed out.

"It's all I've got. I'll have to make the most of it."

"How long will you have to do this dodging-around act?"

Chris shook his head. "I've no idea. Maybe until they get tired, or they change their manner of delivery and no longer use the post office, or something else happens to make them call off the contract."

"Or until they kill Mike or maybe even you, too."

"They're not interested in me."

"As long as you've got Mike and keep them from getting to him, they'll be interested in you," Jennie pointed out.

"I guess that's right," Chris agreed. "But what else can I do?"

Jennie shook her head. "Nothing, I guess. But it's not much of a—a plan."

"I know, but I'm locked in on the things I have to do every day, like going to the base, the post office, coming home. I'll just have to improvise, do things differently every day so they can't catch up with me and hope for the best. I kept them from getting Mike today. I'll have to meet tomorrow when it comes. There are a couple of things I can plan. I can't wait for you and walk home with you anymore. I don't want you in danger if anything happens."

"But we're in this together, remember?"

"Not this part of it. Worrying about Mike is enough.

I don't even want to think what might happen to you if you got caught in this too. So from now on, I can't meet you at the bus stop and walk home with you. Mike and I will have to take a lot of evasive action to avoid those two men."

"Like what?" Jennie asked.

"We can't travel the same route twice in a row. That establishes a pattern and they'd be waiting for us the third time. We'll have to stagger our hours going to the base and leaving the base and going to the post office and leaving the post office. Will you be afraid walking home alone?"

"It's not so bad now. I was really worried those first nights when I followed you and Mike. I'd never walked the seawall alone at night, and it was sort of scary with all the muggings and things I'd heard about. I know now that most of those things happen at the other end of the seawall where it runs into the tough part of the city. So don't worry about me. I'll be all right."

"I'll worry," Chris said. "If anybody starts to follow you, go into the bakery. Bruno'll figure a way to get you home. Or you can call me here at home after twelve-thirty. I should be home by then. I'll come back and get you."

"When will I get to see you?" Jennie asked.

"When Mike and I get home I'll call you. If your father answers, I'll hang up. If you're not home, I'll keep calling until I get you. Don't come over to my place. They might be around watching. And I can't come to your place. We'll just have to talk by phone until this is over." Chris thought of something else and added, "I can't leave Mike here at the houseboat while I go to work at the base anymore. That's the first thing they'll look for."

"I'll come get him. He can stay with me until you get back to pick him up to go to the post office."

Chris shook his head. "That puts you right in the middle of it again. I'll have to take him to the base with me. I think Personnel Officer Sullivan will let me keep him in the mail room. Besides, if you kept him and those two men didn't find him, your father would come home unexpectedly some day and would. Mike has already jumped him once."

"Well, anyway," Jennie said, "it's safe for Mike to stay here with me now while you take the car back. I'll bet those men don't get theirs going again for hours."

"I hope not." Chris rose to leave. "I'll take Andy and Angelina with me and bury them somewhere."

Jennie nodded. "Just don't throw them in a ditch or something like that."

"I won't," Chris said.

On the way into the city, he found a small park of trees. He dug a hole in the soft earth with a stick, put them in, side by side, and built a small cairn of rocks over them. "I'm sorry," he said, "we'll miss you." Then he got into the car and drove away.

Next morning Chris and Mike left for the base a half hour early. They traveled a roundabout way they'd never gone before and saw no one suspicious. In the mail room, Chris tied Mike's leash to the leg of a vacant desk and ordered him to lie down. Mike curled up in the kneehole section of the desk, put his big head on his paws and went to sleep.

Sullivan came through, spotted Mike asleep and grinned. "That's a dog's life? I should have it so good."

"There was no place I could leave him for a couple of days," Chris explained. "I hope you don't mind."

"All right with me," Sullivan said. "Just don't let him get in people's way or kick up a fuss."

"I won't, sir," Chris promised. "Thanks."

That afternoon when he left for the post office, Chris and Mike took another roundabout way that led them a half dozen blocks out of the way. Chris traveled little-used streets so he could watch the people on them and give special attention to any cars that approached. He soon discovered that all he had to do was watch Mike. The dog was trained to be aware of people, sounds and smells. The moment his sharp ears shot forward and he turned his head, Chris knew someone or something was coming close.

They reached the post office without incident and still a half hour early, because he hadn't returned to the houseboat for Mike.

The evening passed quietly. They made their rounds, chased a couple of inquisitive kids away from one of the trucks, and closed some of the outside doors that had been left open. Mike trotted up and down the aisles but found no package that roused his curiosity. When they left, they slipped out a side door and traveled the darkest streets to reach home. Only once did a car seem suspicious. They were some five or six blocks from the post office and hurrying down a dark street when a car came into the block at the corner ahead of them and began moving slowly toward them. They were close to the darkened doorway of some business. Chris pulled Mike into it, discovered a stairway that went deeper, and groped his way down a dozen steps to a landing that was tucked in behind the stairs. It was pitch black. They waited there. A car stopped on the street above. A door slammed. Steps entered the dark doorway. Then they left again. The car door slammed. The car drove off.

At home Chris kept the lights out, sat by the window overlooking the seawall, and watched for Jennie to pass. About ten minutes later she hurried by. He gave her a few minutes to get inside; then he phoned. Her voice said carefully, "Yes?"

"It's me," he said. "We're home."

"How did everything go?" she asked anxiously. "Did you see them or did anyone follow you?"

"Everything went fine. I don't think we were followed, but I'm not sure." He told her about the car and hiding under the dark stairway. "How about you?"

"No problems," Jennie said. "I stopped at the bakery and had a cup of coffee and a doughnut. Bruno wanted to know where you were, and I told him you were working some odd overtime hours filling in for someone else. Was that all right?"

"Sure," Chris said. "I won't be stopping until this is cleared up."

"Chris," Jennie said, "two men came down to your

houseboat this morning and looked around. They didn't try the doors or anything. But they did peek through the windows. I only got a glimpse of those men yesterday, so I couldn't tell much. But one of these men today was sort of tall and slender and he wore glasses. The other was blond and husky, almost fat."

"That's the ones," Chris said.

"They were driving a different car today. It was a red Plymouth sedan."

"They'd change cars since we both got a good look at the other one. How long did they hang around this morning?"

"About half an hour. They walked along the seawall a ways, then got in the car and left. Chris, suppose I called the police and told them a couple of suspicious men were nosing around here."

"All the police could do is ask them a few questions, and you can bet they've got all the right answers prepared. And if you called they'd soon figure that out, and then you could be in trouble. I want you out of this."

"All right, but you be careful," she warned and hung up.

They left an extra half hour early the next morning, took a devious route and arrived at the base without incident. Chris was halfway through the pile of mail and Mike was asleep under the kneehole desk when Lieutenant Ballard came through. He spotted Mike immediately and stopped. "What's he doing here?" he demanded.

Chris explained, "I had no place to leave him, sir. I thought for a couple of days you wouldn't mind if he stayed in here with me. He's very quiet. He doesn't bother anyone. As soon as I can find another place, I won't bring him."

"You won't bring him tomorrow," Ballard said harshly. "He's your private animal, yeoman. This is not a kennel. You keep him off the base. I don't want to come through here again and find him. Understand?"

"Yes, sir," Chris said.

For the rest of the shift, Chris wracked his brain trying to think of a place he could leave Mike. He was getting off shift when it came to him. He went hurrying across the post to Chaplain Holloway's quarters.

Holloway said, "Well, Chris, this is a surprise." He patted Mike's head. "How are you two doing? How is the job going?"

"We're both doing fine, sir, and the job's going well. I'm sorry to be in such a rush, sir, but we're due at the post office in about forty minutes. You've done so much for us already, sir, I hate to ask, but could you help us just once more?"

"That's what I'm here for," Holloway smiled. "What is it?"

"I've been leaving Mike alone at the houseboat while I worked here on base; then I'd pick him up to take him to the post office," Chris explained. "Well, I can't leave him at the houseboat for the next few days, and Lieutenant Ballard won't let him stay in the mail room with me, though he's very quiet and bothers no one. I was wondering if I could leave him with you each day until I get off duty. It'll only be for a few days."

"He hasn't been tearing up the houseboat?" Holloway asked, concerned.

"No, sir, nothing like that. Mike's very good. I just
have to find a place I can leave him for a few days
during the hours I'm on duty here. I'll pick him up
each day when I go to the post office."

"Of course you can leave him," Holloway said. "Is
there anything wrong, Chris?"

"No, sir, nothing wrong. Just a problem I have to
work out. I'll have it taken care of in a few days."

"Good. Then everything is all right," Holloway per-
sisted. "You're not worried about anything?"

"No, sir. Why?"

Holloway's mild eyes studied Chris. "You seem a little uptight, and you look a bit, I don't know, peaked, I
guess."

"I'm fine," Chris insisted. "It's just that I'm holding
down two jobs. I could do with a little more sleep once
in awhile. If it's all right, I'll leave Mike tomorrow
morning about seven-thirty."

"That will be fine." Chaplain Holloway frowned as
he watched Chris and Mike hurry off to their next job.

Once again Chris took a roundabout way to the post
office. There weren't too many people walking in this
section of the city, and he gave each one that came
near a sharp look. And he watched for a red Plymouth
sedan. He was within two blocks of the post office
when a red sedan started around a corner far ahead of
him. Beside him, a door opened in a wall and a man

came out. Chris grabbed the swinging door and jerked Mike inside with him.

They stood in a huge room lined with long benches on which sat dozens of small motors. Some thirty or forty men were working on the motors. A man next to Chris said, "You want something, fella?"

Chris said, "Uh, yes, the office."

"Right through there," the man pointed. "Far end of the building. You came in the service entrance. You'll have to go around the building."

Chris started to walk down between the benches, and the man called, "Hey, you can't go through here!"

Chris pretended not to hear and kept walking fast.

At the far end of the building where the offices were, he turned right, and they were on the street again. They ran the next two blocks to the post office. They had just slipped inside the door when the red Plymouth sedan cruised past. The driver was wearing glasses. Chris could not see the other man.

Again, Chris and Mike spent a quiet evening making their rounds. Several times Chris left Mike in the little room and slipped outside alone and walked completely around the building, looking for the red Plymouth sedan parked in some dark spot, or for someone, loitering in a darkened doorway, or on a street corner, or in the shadows of the building. He saw nothing and no one that could not be accounted for. On the top floor, he opened a window on each side of the building and leaned out and searched the street below and the surrounding buildings and all the dark

113

places. He saw nothing. When the shift changed at midnight, he purposely hung about for another half hour to break the pattern of his and Mike's movements. When they left, he again hunted the darkest streets to reach his own houseboat. Once he thought he saw Jennie, hurrying along ahead of him, but he wasn't sure.

Finally they had to cut back to the seawall and travel along the old dock the last three hundred yards to reach their houseboat. This part worried him most because there was no other approach. They had to travel this distance the same way every night and morning.

Chris stopped behind a lumber pile and studied the distance to his own walkway. There were a number of old lumber piles that he guessed had been here for years. Several boats were upside down on wooden horses. A couple of old motors sat on wooden blocks. There were a dozen places for a man to hide, but he saw nothing unusual. He stepped out holding Mike close on the leash. They almost ran the distance to their walkway. Chris watched Mike's sharp ears for any telltale sign that he'd heard or smelled something unusual. They made it to their walkway and hurried down.

The phone was ringing when he got the door unlocked. It was Jennie. She sounded worried. "Where have you been? This is the third time I've called."

Chris explained that he'd changed his route home and had waited an extra half hour at the post office.

"I was about ready to call the police," she said. "How much longer can you go on dodging them like this? How much longer, Chris?"

"I don't know. As long as I have to. I kept away from them yesterday and I did today. Tomorrow I'll try to do the same thing. It's all I can do."

"There must be something," she insisted. "Somebody you can go to who can stop them."

"Nobody and nothing that won't implicate me, too," Chris said. "If I hadn't destroyed the stuff I found. Even buying the farm has played right into their hands. It's given everybody a reason for making me look guilty. Believe me, Jennie. There isn't anything. I just have to go on doing what I am."

"You're going to run out of things you can do to avoid them," she pointed out. "Then what will you do?"

"I don't know," Chris said. "But I'm not there yet."

"You soon will be."

"Then I'll figure something. Don't worry."

"I can't help worrying."

"I never had anyone worry about me before," Chris said. "I sort of like it."

"I never had anyone to worry about before," Jennie said, "but I don't like it."

Chris said, "I'll call you when I get home tomorrow night."

Jennie's voice turned soft, "You'd better let me call you. Father came home tonight. He's asleep now."

"All right," Chris said.

Chris lay awake looking out the window a long time after his talk with Jennie. She was right. He couldn't go on dodging these men much longer. They were pros at getting rid of people, and he was the rankest kind of amateur. He'd been lucky so far. Very soon now, he'd run out of different dark streets to travel. He could only juggle his time about so much, to confuse them. He was frighteningly close to the end of things he could do—frighteningly close to the end of his rope. Something had better happen to help him, and soon.

He thought seriously of telling Lieutenant Ballard and Captain Wilson. The first thing both would demand was some kind of proof of his story. He hadn't a shred. All he'd accomplish would be to lay himself wide open for more suspicion. He was locked in tight.

Chris looked out the window at the dark water. Beyond, the lights of the city threw a high fan of light into the night sky. But for the soft lap of water against the floats, it was utterly quiet. It was hard to believe he hadn't dreamed all this, that he wouldn't soon wake to find everything had been a horrible nightmare. At the foot of the bed, Mike stretched and sighed. It was true all right. Mike's lying there made it so.

It was sometime later, and he'd been asleep. Mike's low growl and his movement on the bed woke Chris. He lay still a moment, all his faculties suddenly alert. He heard the deep-throated bellow of a freighter boom across the bay, and again the soft lap of water against the floats. The sleepy murmur of a gull came from nearby. Cut it out, Chris told himself. You're getting jumpy. He was about to turn over to try to go back to sleep when, in the faint light from the window, he saw that Mike's head was erect, his sharp ears forward. The growl came again, the faintest rumble deep in his throat. Then Chris heard it. A tiny squeak as weight came down carefully on a loose board of the plank walk.

Chris eased out of bed, patted Mike's big head and whispered, "Quiet, boy. Quiet." He crept to the window and, without disturbing the curtains, peeked out the narrow slit between the two panels of cloth. He was looking straight at the tall, slender figure of a man standing on the porch, not six feet away. Even as he watched, the figure turned his head, and Chris caught the faint glint of eyeglasses.

9

Shock rolled through Chris. His mind raced wildly. For perhaps a minute he did not move. The hit men had finally ventured aboard the houseboat looking for them. The one wearing glasses was watching the bay side of the houseboat where most of the windows were. He wondered where the blond, husky man was. Then he heard the mouselike scratching at the front door. That one was trying to pick the lock. He and Mike were cornered or, he thought quickly, almost. The man wearing glasses could not watch all sides of the house at once. There was a small side door he could not see from his position. It was Mike's and his only chance to get out.

Chris dressed quickly, quietly in the dark, while the dog watched him from the foot of the bed. Then he slipped the leash on Mike, and they padded silently to the small door. Chris eased back the night lock, cracked the door open, then set the night lock again so it would snap shut when he closed the door. He peeked out of the crack. There was no one in sight. He kept a short, tight leash on Mike and stepped outside with the dog crowding beside him. He closed the door softly, and the lock clicked. He stood there trying to think what to do.

The front door lock was a simple one. The blond man would pick it any second. Once inside, they'd know within a minute or two that Chris and Mike were gone. They had to get away from here before that discovery. Chris thought of creeping along the houseboat wall to the walkway. Then when the two men were inside, Mike and he could go up the walkway to the dock. But they'd be in plain sight under the dock light and they couldn't make fast time up the swinging walkway. If they did make it to the top of the dock, there was no place they could get out of sight before those men could follow.

About forty feet away, across the water, was the dark bulk of the dock with its network of pilings. The face of the dock was open, and underneath it was pitch black. If they could get into that blackness, they'd be safe. There was only one way over. Swim.

Chris ducked under the railing, turned and eased himself carefully down into the water, chest-deep. The wave of cold almost took his breath away. He pulled Mike close, whispered, "Come on, boy. Come on." Mike held back. "Hurry up!" Chris pulled on the leash. "Hurry up. We haven't got all day!"

The front door opened with the soft squeak it always

gave out. Chris got an arm around Mike, and holding to the plank walk with the other, he pulled the dog into the water with him. He held the leash in his right hand, turned on his side and began to stroke silently toward the dock.

In the water, Mike thrust out his big head and swam silently beside him, making scarcely a ripple.

"Good boy," Chris whispered. "Good boy."

Chris kept glancing back at the dark windows of the houseboat. The side door opened. The two men stepped outside and stood looking about. That moment Chris's feet touched bottom. He stood motionless, well within the dense shadow of the dock, with just his head above water. He held Mike in his arms and waited. He held his breath for fear Mike would lift a paw and splash or toss his head and disturb the water. In this silence, any little noise would carry to them and draw their attention. But Mike lay as quietly in his arms as if he knew his very life depended upon not moving.

The men stood there for perhaps a minute, looking out at the bay. They looked up at the walkway and the dock above. They were turning to go back inside when there was sudden splashing near Chris and Mike. Both men whirled and looked toward the sound. Chris froze, sure they'd be seen. A gull disturbed by something paddled out of the dark dock shadows and headed across the water toward the houseboat.

"Sea gull," one of the men said disgustedly, "Just a sea gull." They returned inside and closed the door.

Chris waded carefully ashore, carrying Mike. Two piling rows back under the dock, he put the dog down. Mike promptly shook himself and Chris whispered, "Easy. No noise, hear? Quiet, Mike. Quiet."

The tide was out. It was cold and clammy under the dock. Chris was chilled to the bone and could not stop shivering. He held a short leash on Mike and stood behind the second piling from the edge of the dock and watched the dark shape of the houseboat.

After a couple of minutes, the two men came out the front door. The heavyset one fiddled with the lock a few seconds and Chris knew he was carefully locking the door again. Afterward, they stood there talking in low voices. Chris was so close he heard them plainly. "What do you make of this?" the heavyset man asked. "I'd have sworn he came home and didn't leave. But he's gone. He's slick and clean gone. And we watched this houseboat thing, or whatever you call it, every minute."

"You watched it, not me," the man with glasses said. "I left you to watch it while I went to move the car so it'd not be spotted. You sure you kept your eyes on that walkway thing every minute?"

"Every minute."

"No you didn't. When I came back you were looking off up the dock."

"Just for a few seconds."

"More than a few seconds. More like a minute or two. In that time he could come out, go up this walkway and get lost in the dark."

"I don't think so. But even if he could, him and that dog have got to be around here close someplace. Maybe in one of these other houseboats."

"There's about a hundred of these houseboats along here," the man with glasses pointed out. "We're not going to start knocking on doors and asking if a kid and his dog are there."

"If we'd been after a man," the husky one grumbled, "we'd have taken care of him by now and been long gone. I can't figure how this kid and that dog can be so lucky."

"Not lucky—smart," the man with glasses said. "He's outfigured us at every turn. He knows we're after him of course, and he's playing it careful. I've been on these things plenty of times. They always go about the same. Right now he's got the edge. He knows all the streets and alleys and things. He can jiggle his time coming and going. But that edge won't last long because we'll be learning those same streets and we'll know the times he can come and go. Then we can do some planning, too. He'll run out of different ways to go and different times. Then he'll have to start repeating himself. Eventually he'll make a mistake. That's when we catch up with him. One thing you can always count on; time's working for us. Not him."

"So what do we do now?"

"We wait right here to see if he shows." They sat down against the wall of the houseboat, well back in the shadows, and lapsed into silence.

Chris became cold and began to shiver. It looked

like the two men meant to stay for several hours. There was no use watching them. He moved farther back under the dock, tied Mike's leash to a crossbeam, ordered him again to be still, then began rubbing his arms and legs trying to restore circulation. It didn't seem to help. He wanted to sit down, but the sand was soggy underfoot because the tide flooded in here. He leaned against a slimy piling and continued to shiver. He wrapped his arms tight about himself to hold the little heat in his body. Numbness began seeping into him. He crept stealthily to the outside edge of the dock and looked at the houseboat. The two men were black blobs sitting against the wall. He returned to Mike and leaned against the piling. There was nothing to do but to wait until the men left.

Chris had no watch, but finally he knew it was getting close to dawn. The black surface of the bay began to fade. The distant lights of the city were less bright. He watched the approaching day push the night back beyond the surrounding hills. The city's skyline appeared. Then the dawn seemed to explode into the sky. But the sun had not yet come. The moment it did, Chris realized, it would flood in under the dock and make everything visible. Then a second problem presented itself. The tide was coming in. It was already lapping at the base of the second piling and coming fast. If those men stayed, in another half hour he'd be standing in a foot of water. By eight o'clock, when he had to be at the base, he'd be swimming. Chris crept to the outer edge of the dock for another look at the two men. In this new light, he could see them now, hunched up in their coats, knees pulled up. There was no indication that they meant to leave anytime soon. Mike and he had to find a way out of here, and they had to do it before full day struck.

Chris untied Mike and they began threading their way among the forest of pilings, looking for some way out. They passed another walkway and a houseboat. A hundred feet beyond, they came to a cross wall made of heavy planks nailed to the pilings. The wall extended to the very outer edge of the dock. They had to get around this wall. That meant wading right out into the open beyond the protection of the dock.

Chris looked toward his houseboat. He could see a corner of it beyond the one they'd just passed. The two men were standing now, their backs to him as they looked at something down the long line of houseboats. If they hurried, they might get around this wall before they turned back.

Chris took a short grip on Mike's leash and waded carefully into the water. Mike followed dutifully and began to swim when Chris was just slightly above his knees. Chris kept looking back toward the two men while he waded. He was chest-deep when he finally rounded the end of the wall. A minute later, they were out and hiking among the pilings again. But this time, the wall hid them from the two men.

They passed several walkways and houseboats, but they found no way up onto the dock until they'd gone almost a hundred yards. Then they came in to a narrow stairway that led up through a hole in the dock floor. They climbed the stairs and, at the top, Chris looked back toward his houseboat. Several others completely hid it from sight. They hurried across the dock and in among a maze of old lumber piles that had been here for years. They almost ran into the red Plymouth sedan parked behind one of the piles. Chris was tempted to rip the wiring out of this car too. But that would let them know he'd been hiding somewhere close by.

Chris was looking about for a place to hide when he heard feet coming along the dock. He peeked around the corner of the lumber pile, and there were the two men, not fifty feet away.

Chris and Mike scurried to the next lumber pile and crouched down behind it. Chris held Mike close and put his hand over his nose. He heard one say, "It'll be full light in less than an hour. He won't be coming back. And we don't want to be seen around here any more than necessary, especially not in the early morning, when people are heading out to work. There'll be another time." They got into the car and drove away.

Chris and Mike came out from behind the lumber pile and headed up the dock toward their own houseboat. Chris's muscles were stiff. The cold seemed to have gone completely through him. Mike trotted beside him, as if this whole episode had been some kind of game that he'd enjoyed.

Aboard the houseboat, Chris learned the two men were careful to disturb nothing. There was just time to change into dry clothes, get something to eat, feed Mike, and put up his lunch for the post office that night.

When he delivered Mike to Chaplain Holloway at the base, the little man looked closely at him and said, "You're sure there isn't something you'd like to tell me, Chris?"

"No, sir," Chris said.

Holloway nodded. "Just remember, if there's anything I can do, don't hesitate to say so. Unraveling problems is part of my job."

"Yes, sir," Chris said. "I'll remember. Thanks for keeping Mike for me. I'll pick him up as soon as I get off duty."

The moment he walked into the mail room, Sullivan said, "Man, you look like you've had a night. What happened to you?"

"Couldn't sleep."

"That's all?"

"That's all," Chris answered.

Lieutenant Ballard came through a little later, looked sharply at Chris, but said nothing. While he worked, Chris thought of last night and the two men. The words of the man with glasses kept running through his mind, like the fatal ticking of a time bomb. "Eventually he'll make a mistake. That's when we catch up with him. . . . Time's working for us. Not him." Again he thought seriously of going to Lieutenant Ballard and laying the story before him. But when he thought of the lieutenant's sharp, hard fea-

126

tures and cold, impersonal eyes, he knew he couldn't do it. There'd be no sympathy there.

When Chris picked up Mike at Chaplain Holloway's quarters and headed for the post office, he tried to be very careful. He searched the length of each street before he entered, and he paid particular attention to doorways, stairwells, or any other places that would serve as hiding spots if they had to duck for cover in a hurry. He said once to Mike trotting ahead of him, tail waving, sharp ears jumping back and forth as they picked up a variety of sounds, "If anybody had told me I'd do all these crazy things just for a dog, I'd have said 'No way.' " Mike glanced back at the sound of his voice, and Chris finished with a smile, "But you're worth it." With all his precautions, they arrived at the post office fifteen minutes ahead of time and without incident.

During the evening, Chris planned some different way to go home that would throw the men off track. They'd expect Mike and him to walk, but to take some different street. Therefore, they'd not walk. Fifteen minutes before the end of the shift, he called a cab company and ordered a cab to meet them in the post office truck lot.

When the cab pulled up beside them, the driver scowled out the window at Mike, "You didn't say nothing about no dog."

"What's the difference?" Chris said. "He's clean. He's neat. He'll cause no trouble."

"I don't make a practice of carrying dogs, except

maybe one of them tiny poodles that only weighs a couple of pounds. This fellow's a regular elephant."

"Then this can be a first." Chris smiled. "This dog is special."

"They're all special," the driver grumbled. "I got one of these bruisers myself. All right, get in."

Chris had the driver go down the line of houseboats almost to the end, before they got out. When Chris paid him, he indicated Mike with a jerk of his head. "Your friend's a real gentleman all right, which is more than I can say for a lot of people I carry. You want to take him again, just tell the dispatcher to call Sam."

"I'll do that," Chris said. "Thanks." Mike and he followed the taxi up the dock to their houseboat.

Chris was sure that since they had eluded the two men by taking the cab, that they would soon realize they'd been tricked and would head for the houseboat. Inside he was careful not to disturb anything from the way it had been last night. He got a spare blanket from a closet, and Mike and he left the houseboat again. They went back down the dock to the area of the old lumber piles. He found a small pile about four feet high and beside it another almost eight feet. He lifted Mike to the smaller one, followed him up and boosted the dog to the high one and climbed up after him. He spread the blanket, lay down on it and pulled Mike down beside him. "Keep your head down," he warned. "If they see us up here we're goners." From here he had a good view of the dock even in the dark, and he could clearly see the light over his own walk-way. Anyone going down it would be plainly visible. He had chosen this spot for another reason: up here in the air would be the last place they'd look for Mike and him.

They had been there but a few minutes when head-lights washed the dock and the Plymouth sedan stopped a short distance off. The two men got out, walked swiftly along the dock and went down his walkway. The moment they entered the deep dark under the porch, they were hidden from Chris's view. He lay quiet and waited. He thought he saw the brief probe of a flashlight beam through the curtains, but he wasn't sure. No lights were turned on, but he knew they were inside checking the house over.

After a few minutes, the two men returned. They walked quietly, making no noise with their feet, and then Chris realized they both wore sneakers. They re-ally meant business, he thought.

They were talking quietly as they walked up to their car. The heavyset one said, "Everything's just as it was when we were here last night. Bed's not even been made, nothing. And he'd make the bed from sheer habit. That's the first thing a coastguardsman does every morning, make his bed. I know."

The one wearing glasses said, "He's not living here now, that's for sure. It's logical too. He may even be staying a different place every night so we can't get a line on him and set a trap."

"Then what do we do?"

"No sense coming down here anymore. Since we don't know where he's sleeping, we can't intercept him going to the Coast Guard base. Going from the base to the post office, and when he leaves the post office at midnight, is our best bet. Especially the first few blocks when he leaves the post office. He has to pull out of the post office at midnight, and for the first few blocks he doesn't have many different ways to go. That's what we're going to start concentrating on. I've got a feeling we're going to catch up with him pretty soon."

They got into the car and drove away.

Chris and Mike came down off the lumber pile and returned to the houseboat. He was careful to keep the place dark so it would continue to look as if no one was home. He groped his way to the phone and called Jennie.

Her voice came, frightened and almost tearful, "Chris! Chris, you all right?"

"Of course," he said. "Why?"

"I called a few minutes ago and a strange man's voice answered. Chris was he one of—of them?"

"Yes," Chris answered. "I thought they might come here looking for us, so Mike and I hid on top of a lumber pile until they left."

"They broke into the house to look for you!" Jennie's voice was climbing. She was near panic.

"They didn't break in; they picked the lock. They were very careful. They didn't disturb a thing. They're not looking for me, really. It's Mike they want."

"It doesn't make any difference. You're with Mike and you're keeping him away from them, so they're after you, too. Chris, you can't go on sneaking around this way any longer. You've got to go to the police before something terrible happens."

"Just don't panic," Chris soothed. "Mike and I are doing all right. They think Mike and I aren't living here anymore, so they won't be looking here for us We're safe here as long as we're careful."

"Safe for how long?" Jennie asked. "How long, Chris? You call this dodging around the way you are being safe? You're not facing facts, Chris."

"Yes I am," Chris insisted. "I know what will happen the minute I go to the police. That's a last resort. If I do I lose everything, everything! Do you understand? I'm trying to save something for us, too."

Jennie didn't answer for a long minute. Then she said in a frightened, subdued voice, "I wish there was something I could do."

"There is," Chris said, "don't worry. I'll call you tomorrow night."

After he hung up, Chris literally fell into bed. He felt safe here for the first time in days. He was asleep so fast he wasn't aware when Mike crawled up on the foot of the bed and stretched out with a gusty sigh.

10

Caution had become a way of life with Chris. Before they left the houseboat next morning, he carefully studied the length of dock he could see, and finding nothing, he then walked as far as the nest of old lumber piles and looked for the red Plymouth sedan. The man with glasses had said they'd no longer look for them at the houseboat, but Chris knew that all they needed was a grain of suspicion and they'd be back. So this morning, he used all his caution.

They took a roundabout way to get to the base. It was longer, more time-consuming, but it felt safer than any of the others. They arrived at the base with very little time to spare. When he left Mike with Chaplain Holloway, the little man smiled at him and observed, "Everything is a little better this morning, Chris?"

"Yes, sir, much better," Chris said.

"Good," he said. "Good."

Even Sullivan commented that he must have gotten a good night's sleep, and Chris agreed.

The day in the mail room passed as it always did. Chris dished out mail, received mail, and sold stamps and money orders, and weighed packages. Lieutenant Ballard came through once. He scowled at Chris but didn't speak. Sullivan said later, "Got a lot on his mind, I guess."

When Chris picked up Mike and headed for the post office, he became extremely cautious again. This was one of the areas the man with glasses had said they'd concentrate on. This time Chris took a route he'd never traveled before. It was so little used there was only one car parked along a whole three-block length. It was a street of expensive condominiums and apartments and was obviously rarely traveled by anyone but the people who lived there. It ran parallel to the direction he wanted to go. He could see any car that came into the street at least two blocks away.

Mike and he hurried the full length of the street, and Chris saw no one and no car came into view. He followed the street to within two blocks of the post office. Then they cut through a narrow alley and came out within half a block of the post office. A minute later, they were inside the building. They were ten minutes early.

Chris went to the far end of the building where there was a small, frosted window that looked out on the street. He cracked the window open and stood watching the street. He hadn't been there more than a couple of minutes when the red Plymouth sedan cruised slowly past. That was close, he thought, too close.

All evening Chris thought of how to avoid the two men. Getting away from the post office was going to be the biggest problem. Once he was four or five blocks away, he could choose any one of a half dozen different streets to get to the houseboat. He thought of staying around here and leaving later, but they would be on to that now. He couldn't leave earlier. He had to wait for his replacement, Lou West, at midnight. He might call the cab again. But they were watching the post office very closely and they'd be suspicious of any cab pulling in here for a fare at midnight. At eleven o'clock, Mike and he were standing outside. Chris was looking the length of the loading dock and watching a couple of trucks loading up with mail for a run out of the city when the solution for getting away came to him. He walked down to the first truck and asked the driver, "How soon you leaving?"

"Two or three minutes," the driver said.

Chris went on to the next truck and asked the same question. "Soon as I finish loading out," the driver said. "Maybe ten, fifteen minutes. You in a hurry to close these doors?"

"Just wondered," Chris said and strolled away.

Chris kept watching the loading dock for trucks, but this time of night, the big rush was over. A truck rolled in at eleven-thirty, but this one came to unload and would be left for the night in the truck lot. It was a quarter to twelve when a lone truck pulled in to load out. Chris talked to the driver. "When you leaving?"

"Soon as I get loaded. About twelve."

"How about Mike and me riding out with you a little ways?"

"We ain't supposed to take riders." The driver adjusted his cap and smiled. "Heck, you work here. Okay."

Chris and Mike were standing on the dock watching the last of the loading when the shift changed. Five minutes later, they pulled out. Chris and Mike rode in the cab with the driver.

"Sing out when you want to get off," the driver said. "I got to hit the expressway in a few blocks."

They traveled four blocks and Chris was alert for the red Plymouth sedan. He saw nothing. At a corner, the driver turned right and said, "This's where I head for the freeway."

"We'll get off at the next corner," Chris said, "and thanks for the lift."

After alighting from the truck, Chris stood a minute while he got his bearings. The area looked familiar even in the dark. Then it came to him where they were. They were at the head of the street of condominiums and expensive apartments that they'd walked this afternoon. They could follow it a couple of blocks; then they'd have to cut to the left for about three blocks, which would bring them into the warehouse and seawall area that led to the houseboat.

They crossed the street and began to walk. Mike's

head came up, his ears shot forward and he twisted around. That moment they were hit by headlights from behind. Chris glanced over his shoulder, but all he saw were blinding headlights bearing down on them fast.

Warning yelled through him. He yanked on the leash and said harshly, "Mike, come on! Come!" He turned right, raced across a lawn toward an apartment, and was momentarily out of the light beam into the dark again. They were at the corner of an apartment building when tires screamed behind them. Chris heard a car door open and slam, then running feet.

They dashed the length of the building, came to a low fence that Mike and he jumped easily, and raced on. At the end of each apartment, they found the same low fence separating the yards. They sailed over each one without slackening speed.

The fourth yard brought them to the end of the block. Chris stopped in the shadow of the last apartment and looked back. At first he saw no one. Then far back, the shape of a man moved through a yard, peeking into shrubbery and around corners. He did not see the second man.

Chris checked the length of the cross street. It was empty. For the few seconds it would take to cross, they'd be out in the open. But there was nothing else for it. He said, "Come on, Mike," and running on his toes so as to make no noise, they dashed across and into the next backyard. The man behind was not coming fast, so Chris slowed down and tried to think. They

136

had about two more blocks of this street; then they'd come into a more lighted district. They had to lose these men before they reached that light. He wondered briefly where the second man was.

As they ran, Chris kept looking about for someplace to hide. He studied the windows, hoping for a lighted one that would say someone was still up, and he could knock on the door and ask for help. If he tried a house that was dark, it would be several minutes as least before anyone came to the door. He couldn't wait that long. He found no hiding place except the low, well-kept shrubs that the man behind was carefully combing through.

They jumped the last fence and entered the last yard at the end of the block That moment the Plymouth sedan pulled up to the curb and the lights were turned off. The heavyset man got out and started toward them. Chris knew what had happened. One had started chasing him two blocks back. This one had come on with the car to get ahead of him and box him in, and they had.

Chris looked frantically at the dark bulk of the house he was about to pass. He saw a wall jutting out from the house to form a little enclosed courtyard where a family could enjoy privacy from the eyes of their neighbors. There was a wooden gate in the middle of the wall. Chris ran to the gate hoping it was unlocked. It was. He opened it. They slipped inside and he closed it. They were in a little yard about ten feet square. There was no place to hide. You went directly into the house from here. The searching man behind would certainly look in the yard.

Chris's mind was racing. He was surprised how clearly he was thinking. He had about a minute. They were going to be seen. He had to do something, and whatever it was, it had to be bold and startling to throw them off track. They'd never gotten a closeup look at him in daylight. They'd seen him once at night when they tried to run Mike down. That had been a short, quick glimpse in the dark. They'd seen him once in daylight, out at the farm. That had been more than a hundred yards away and they'd seen only his back. Tonight they'd glimpsed him in the headlight beam for an instant, from more than a hundred feet away, and again in the dark. He knew then what he had to do. There was no time to think or plan, only to act.

He tied Mike short to one of the fence posts in the yard and told him to be quiet. Swiftly he stripped off his shirt with its Coast Guard insignia, rolled his bell-bottom pants, which were a dead giveaway, halfway to his knees, and boldly stepped out of the gate, closed it and walked straight toward the dark shape of the heavyset man. To his left, Chris glimpsed the slender shape of the man with the glasses just climbing the last fence into the yard.

The heavyset man saw him coming and stopped uncertainly. Chris had to swallow twice before his voice would come natural. Then he said, "You sure got here in a hurry, but you missed him."

The man said uncertainly, "What?"

"The guy I phoned you about," Chris said. "You are from the police, aren't you?"

The man with the glasses came up and looked at him closely. He pushed the glasses up on his nose and said, "Police? Oh, yeah, sure. Sure."

"Well," Chris rushed on, "I was getting ready for bed and I heard some kind of noise and looked out the window. I live right here." He waved at the dark house. "I saw this guy come into the yard with the big dog. I came out and he took off. I chased him a little way but I didn't even try to get close. That big dog didn't look too friendly. We don't like strangers wandering around the yard in the middle of the night. I came back to the house and called the police." He looked at the sedan parked at the curb and said, "I thought they'd send a prowl car."

"Detectives," the glasses man said. "We took the call and were in the neighborhood." He kept looking at Chris. "Which way did you say he went?"

"Off across there," Chris pointed. "The next street over."

"You look sort of familiar," the glasses man said.

"Could be," Chris agreed. "If you've ever stopped by the Tick Tok, I'm the night cook there."

"Just getting home?"

Chris nodded. "About to go to bed when I heard the noise and saw the fellow."

"House looks pretty dark."

"I live with my folks," Chris said glibly. "I try to be quiet so I won't wake them."

"You get a good look at this fellow and dog?"

"Only from the back and in the dark. The dog was big. I'd guess he was a police dog. The fellow must have been young the way he ran. Sort of slim, about my height, I'd guess."

"How far did you chase them?"

"Just out of the yard and a little way across the street."

"How long do you figure before we got here?"

Chris considered, "Not more than a couple of minutes. I hardly got back outside when you drove up."

The man with glasses looked around again. He was suspicious but Chris's answers were too logical. Finally he said to the other man, "Let's go." They left Chris and walked back to their car.

Chris said, "If I spot him again, I'll call in."

"You do that," the glasses man said. They got into the car and drove off.

Chris waited until they were out of sight; then he ran back inside the gate, slipped into his shirt, rolled down his pants, untied Mike and they left in a hurry.

They ran straight across the street, cut back toward the waterfront for three blocks and came into the warehouse area again. There they turned right, still running, and raced along in the shadows of the warehouses. They traveled some distance. Then it came to Chris that they had come to no cross street. He remembered from that afternoon the street of condominiums and apartment houses was only three blocks long. He'd covered two blocks when the two men cornered him in the yard. That left one more block, and it was a dead end with no cross street. The one with glasses, already suspicious, would ask himself how Chris, living there, could make such a mistake. By now he'd have the answer. The young, half-dressed man he'd been talking to was the one they were looking for. They'd be combing this area again any minute.

They came to an old warehouse with rows of broken windows. Chris guessed it was empty. He found a door and tried it. It was unlocked. They went inside and closed the door. Chris found a crack in the wooden wall and glued his eye to it and watched the street. They had been there perhaps ten minutes when the Plymouth sedan cruised past, going slow. They waited, and a few minutes later it passed again, going in the opposite direction. Chris guessed another half hour passed, but he saw nothing. Those men would probably figure that Mike and he were a long way from here by now.

Chris decided it was safe to return to the houseboat. The glasses man had said last night that they'd no longer watch it, and tonight when they'd been cornered, they had been heading toward the heart of the city.

Chris and Mike approached the houseboat area cautiously, taking no chances. There was no Plymouth sedan anywhere, no sight of the two men. They went down the swinging walkway and entered. Chris groped his way to the phone in the dark and called Jennie. Her voice was anxious and frightened, "Where have you been? I've called and called. You're an hour later than usual."

"We came home a different way. It took longer. Anything happen here?"

"No," she said. "It's been quiet. How about with you?"

"Nothing," Chris lied. "Everything's going all right."

"I hate it." Chris could hear the fear in her voice. "This not knowing what's going to happen next. What's going to be the end, Chris? This can't go on much longer."

"It won't," he said. "Believe me, Jennie."

Mike made a sound in his throat. Chris glanced at him. His ears were erect. He was looking out the slit of window between the curtain panels. Chris glanced out and his heart gave a tremendous leap and began to race madly. At the edge of the circle of light at the head of the walkway and looking down at the houseboat, stood the two men. He whispered into the phone, "Jennie, I've got to hang up. Those two men are here. They're standing on the dock right by the walkway. I'll call later." Her voice was calling his name fearfully as he hung up.

Chris dragged Mike back from the window and whispered, "Quiet, Mike! Not a sound. Quiet!" Then he sat there and tried to think. The first thing that ran through his mind were the words of the man who wore glasses. "Eventually he'll make a mistake. That's when we catch up with him."

Tonight he'd made that mistake when he came back

here. Why it was a mistake, he didn't know. But then he was an amateur and they were professionals. Especially the one who wore glasses. He knew how a hunted man thought, the things he'd do, and apparently Chris had done exactly what he expected.

If only he had a gun, a weapon of some kind. But he knew there was nothing here. Then he'd fight with whatever he could get his hands on. There was a heavy chair in the kitchen. He tiptoed in and got it. He unsnapped the leash from Mike's collar. Maybe he'd attack one of them. At least he'd have freedom to move. He took up a position beside the front door. It would be dark in here. When they opened the door, he'd get at least one good swing. From then on he'd have to play it by ear.

There was a window beside the door. He peeked through the curtains and watched them. They were starting down the walkway, moving carefully because they were not used to the swinging. Coolness went through Chris like a breeze. This was it. He quit thinking.

For days they'd been running and hiding and ducking, trying to outwit and stay ahead of these two men. In the next minute or so it would be over. Maybe they'd kill Mike, even him too. Maybe they wouldn't. But one thing he knew: the first man through this door was going to get a headache he'd never forget.

Suddenly the walkway was bathed in light from a big flood next door. Through the curtains he saw the whole houseboat light up. He could see a corner of the

143

houseboat beyond, and lights had come on there. The whole dock was lit up, bright as day.

Halfway down the walkway the two men stopped uncertainly. Then Jennie strolled along the dock and to his walkway and began talking to the men. She still wore her drive-in uniform.

The two men went back up the walkway to her. They stood there for several minutes. Jennie did most of the talking. She waved her arms, encompassing the whole dock and line of houseboats. She pointed. Once she even laughed. The two men nodded agreeably. The one pushed his glasses up on his nose and patted her on the shoulder. Then they walked away.

Jennie leaned against the walkway cable for perhaps five minutes. Then she ran down the walkway and hammered on the door. "Chris," she cried, "they're gone! They're gone!"

Chris opened the door and she was in his arms sobbing, "Oh, Chris, I was so frightened I thought I'd die."

Chris held her close until she stopped crying, and then he asked, "What happened? All the lights coming on? Everything?"

In the dark Jennie wiped her eyes and blew her nose. "When you hung up I started calling all the other houseboats. I told them to turn on all the lights they had because there was a couple of undesirable men about. They're all friends of mine. We've had trouble with things being stolen. So they all did. I thought if there was lots of light they'd be afraid to try anything, and they were."

144

"I saw you come over and talk to them. You even laughed once. What was all that about?"

"I had to laugh," Jennie said. "I was frightened to death but I had to pretend they were just people. They said they were friends of yours and were looking for you. I told them you'd left a couple of days ago and I didn't know where you were. I was sort of keeping an eye on the place while you were gone. I played it real dumb."

"Real smart I'd say," Chris said admiringly. "Didn't the lights make them suspicious?"

"I told them the truth about that, missing things and turning on the lights when strangers wandered around here at night. They thought it was pretty clever." Jennie changed the subject abruptly and Chris could feel her eyes boring into him in the dark. "What now, Chris? What will you do next? Didn't this tell you something? It was awfully close."

It was too close, and Jennie's actions a few minutes ago had now gotten her involved. She was right. He could no longer protect Mike. There was only one avenue left open to him now. Lay the whole story before Lieutenant Ballard. He knew how rough the lieutenant would be on him. He'd be kicked out of the Coast Guard with a dishonorable discharge. That meant he'd lose the farm for sure and the job he'd meant to go to at the end of his hitch. But he'd save Mike and after what happened here tonight, he'd be saving Jennie too. That was the important thing. He said, "Tomorrow morning I'll tell Lieutenant Ballard everything and let him take it from there."

"He'll get those men off your back? Everything will be all right?" Jennie asked.

"Everything will be fine," Chris said. "You'll see. Now you'd better get out of here, just in case, and tell the neighbors thanks for turning on their lights."

"Just in case what?" Jennie asked.

"I don't know, but these are dangerous men. Just in case." He pulled her into his arms and kissed her hard. "I couldn't stand it if anything happened to you." Jennie would have clung to him but he pushed her toward the door. "You'd better get going."

Jennie hesitated. "Chris, even if telling Ballard means losing the farm like you said, we can get another."

"Sure." He watched her run lightly up the walkway and disappear. A minute later the lights began winking out.

Chris sat down in the kitchen chair. He was tired. He felt drained out and discouraged and helpless. Mike came and put his big head in his hands. Chris patted him and said, "We gave it the big try anyway. It just didn't work out. I'm sorry, Mike. I'm truly sorry."

11

Chris slept little that night. All through the long, dark hours he thought of his decision to tell Lieutenant Ballard everything and what it would mean to him. He tried to think of some way to ease the telling so he wouldn't appear quite so guilty. There was none. He hadn't done anything right. "You're going to get it," he told himself, "make up your mind to that." He hadn't the faintest idea where he'd go or what he'd do once he was kicked out of the service. He'd have to meet that problem when he came to it.

As soon as it was light, he dressed, put up a lunch and made breakfast. Then he sat and looked at the food with no desire to eat. He fed it to Mike and watched him gobble it down. He washed the dishes, made the bed, and then walked through the house making sure everything was in place. He liked it here but after today he'd not be able to stay. Just another problem he'd have to meet when he was kicked out of the service.

Jennie thought that all he'd lose would be the farm. There would be a lot of other things. He wondered what she'd say to some of them. Maybe she wouldn't want to see him again. He wouldn't have much to offer after today. Another problem, he told himself.

The sun was lancing across the bay. The day was full. They were ready to leave for the base. Chris reminded himself to be extremely careful. These men had a very good line on him now, the way he came and went, the routes he took. Even the way he thought. He'd do something different this morning. He called the cab company and asked if Sam was still on shift. He worked graveyard. He still had an hour to go.

Twenty minutes later the cab pulled up at the head of the walkway. Sam said, "How's your big friend this morning?" He patted Mike on the head. "Get in, pal."

He left Mike with Chaplain Holloway. For a moment he was tempted to tell the little chaplain his problems, then changed his mind. In this situation, no one could help. The facts were there. They could not be twisted by anyone. There was no use putting Holloway in an awkward position.

"Anything wrong, Chris?" Holloway asked.

Chris shook his head, "No, nothing," and left.

All morning Chris waited for Lieutenant Ballard to come through. But today it was almost two o'clock before the lieutenant put in an appearance. He came through, walking very fast, his lean, chiseled features looking sharper, harder than usual. Chris said, "Lieutenant, I'd like to talk to you a minute."

"What?"—Ballard swung toward him—"What'd you say?"

"Is there someplace private where we can talk, sir?"

"No," Ballard snapped, "there's not."

"But, sir, this is important," Chris insisted.

Ballard faced him then, shoulders squared, chin out. "Yeoman," his voice was cutting, "nothing you could ever say to me would be important. Get that straight once and for all." Then he whirled and marched out.

Chris looked at Sullivan surprised. Sullivan said, "He's pretty uptight all right."

"About what?" Chris asked.

"Haven't you heard? They got a tip that a big shipment of dope is coming in sometime tonight on a freighter. Ballard's taking a squad down to search it. This time he'd better find it. Two misses in a row would look mighty bad for his drug-bust program. In fact, it could just about knock him out of it, and he knows it."

Chris had worked himself up to it. Now he wanted to get it over with. He said, "How about me taking off a few minutes early today. I'd like to see Captain Wilson."

"Sure," Sullivan said, "but Captain Wilson's gone. He won't be back until sometime tomorrow. That's what's making it so tough on Ballard. It throws the whole responsibility on him."

Chris felt disappointed, but underneath there was a small satisfaction that he had one more day's grace. He'd have to continue being careful this afternoon when he went to the post office, when he left at midnight, and when he returned to the base tomorrow morning. He'd make that easy, he told himself.

He made it to the post office with no trouble, simply by doubling back on his route and taking the one he'd gone over the first day.

The evening went quietly. They made their rounds, Mike trotting importantly ahead of Chris. Some of the people talked to him, petted him, and kidded Chris, wondering where the dog was taking the man. This night, Chris didn't even have to chase anyone away from the line of parked trucks.

All evening Chris planned ways they could leave the post office and reach the houseboat without the two men seeing them, and one by one he discarded each plan. They couldn't leave again in one of the mail trucks. Those men had evidently followed the truck because they picked them up so quickly. Calling Sam, the cabdriver, was out. They'd been lucky twice. Three times would be pushing it too much.

Chris reviewed in his mind the different routes they'd taken in the past. There were no new ones left. He tried to think as those men would. Then he remembered the seawall. They hadn't gone that way since the first night when the two men tried to run Mike down. They'd figure he was afraid to take it because there weren't many places to hide. And he admitted to himself, he was. Then that was the way to cross them up. But this time they'd keep to the deep shadows of the warehouses, and wherever there was a light, they'd detour around it even if it meant going a couple of blocks out of the way. It would take a lot longer, but this was the last night they'd have to do it.

Lou West, his replacement, came in fifteen minutes early and Chris said, "Can you take over now? I've got something I have to do."

West lifted a hand. "See you tomorrow night."

They were fifteen minutes ahead of the shift change, Chris thought. That should throw those two vultures off stride.

The end of the first block, they turned right down a narrow street. They walked another block and were at the back side of the string of warehouses that fronted on the seawall. They'd never gone down this particular street before because it seemed more like an alley. The walls of the buildings were blank with few doors and no windows. These were truly the backs of the buildings where no one came and nothing was done to make them inviting.

They traveled the first block, crossed the street and were halfway down the second block when Mike's head came up, his ears shot forward and he swung halfway around to look behind. A sedan had pulled up at the mouth of the street, and the bulk of a man was getting out. He didn't have to see the color of the car or the glasses the man wore to know they were in deeper trouble than they'd been last night. They'd pulled the same old trick on him and there was no way he could have avoided it. He took a short grip on the leash and said to Mike, "Come on, run! Let's go!"

They raced to the corner. There Chris turned left, toward the bay. Afterward he was never sure why he'd turned left instead of right except that the street was a gentle downhill slope and he could run faster downhill than up. He needed every ounce of speed he could muster.

At the end of the block, he glanced back. The slender man wearing glasses was rounding the corner and sprinting after him. The second man was not in sight.

At the end of the next block, he came suddenly to the seawall and the black, quiet expanse of the bay. He had to turn right or left. He turned right and kept running at top speed.

Where he came from, Chris never knew. But suddenly, there ahead of him in the dark, the heavyset man was waiting. Chris skidded to a stop. Mike pulled on the leash, his sharp ears forward, looking at the man. Chris turned to go back but the man behind was closing fast.

There was only one place left to go and he took it. Across the seawall and down a way, the dark slab of Bruno's bakery spilled a square of light into the street. Chris jerked on the leash. Mike and he raced across the street and headed for the light. If there were people in the bakery, the men wouldn't dare enter and try anything.

They had no trouble outrunning the clumsy, heavy-set man.

The front part of the bakery was empty. Chris dashed around the counter into the big back room. Here thousands of loaves of bread and pastries of all kinds waited on long metal shelves for delivery to retail bakeries and stores. Inside the door, they almost ran into Bruno.

Bruno, as always, was in a thin undershirt and he wore the white hat with his name on it, perched on the back of his bald head. Flour was dusted across his fat face and thick bare arms. "Whoa, there, stranger," he laughed, "where you going in such a rush?"

"You got a back door to this room?" Chris panted. "Where is it?"

"Sure there's a back door, side door, really. It's where the trucks load out. They'll be coming in soon."

"Show me. We've got to get out of here quick. There's some men chasing us."

Bruno was maddeningly slow. "Chasing you?" he asked. "What for?"

"They're out to kill Mike," Chris threw at him annoyed. "Where's the back door, Bruno? Quick!"

"Come off it," Bruno laughed. "Your imagination's getting the best of you. You've been seeing too many gangster movies. Anybody comes in here I'll handle 'em. Relax." He took Chris's arm to lead him out into the other room. "Come on," he said soothingly, "I'll get you a cup of coffee and a doughnut. That'll fix you right up. It always has."

Chris jerked his arm free and started down an aisle looking for a door. The next moment Bruno grabbed his arm in an iron grip and swung him around. "Take it easy, friend. Nobody, but nobody, goes wandering through here unless I say so." Chris stared at the fat baker with shocked surprise. That tough voice and manner was something new.

The next moment the two men burst through the door and were in the room with them. Both brandished guns.

"Well," the heavyset one wheezed noisily, "you gave us quite a run, sonny."

Mike began to growl. The heavyset man pointed his gun at him and Bruno said sharply, "Not here, you fool!"

The one wearing glasses pushed them up on his nose and said to Bruno, "Now what do we do? We couldn't help it that he busted in here."

"Don't worry about it." Bruno still held Chris's arm in a viselike grip. "It'll work out."

"If we get rid of the dog," the glasses man pointed out, "what about the kid? Our orders were not to touch him."

"I gave those orders. We're going to change them right now," Bruno said. "He goes along with the dog. Make it a long ways from here. Understand?"

Chris was dumbfounded. He could not believe what he was hearing. Bruno, the fat, good-natured baker, with flour on his face and arms, who dished out coffee and doughnuts and petted Mike and was so friendly with Jennie, was part of the mob! Part of it! As the incredible words sank into Chris's numb mind, he realized that Bruno was giving the orders. It was Bruno who'd put out the contract on Mike.

Bruno was talking to him in the old friendly voice. "Your big mistake, Chris, was coming in here the first night."

Chris didn't answer. He clung tight to Mike's leash, and thoughts leapfrogged through his mind. Maybe they could still break loose and run for it. But the heavyset man stood in the doorway to the shop at the front of the bakery. The gun in his hand was pointed at Chris's chest. The other way, into the big bakery and storage room, was blocked by Bruno, who still held his arm, and the slender man with glasses who also held a gun pointed at Chris.

Bruno was talking again. Now his voice was deadly and businesslike. "Get the car. Bring it to the side door and take both of them out of here. I don't want to see either of them again. Understand?"

"You won't."

But as the heavyset man put his gun away, there was a sudden commotion in the shop. The next moment a group of people boiled through the door. The heavyset man was struggling in the arms of two burly coastguardsmen. Another coastguardsman and Lieutenant Ballard were with them. Behind the little group was Jennie, brown eyes popping, lips parted as if about to scream with fright. The man with glasses started to swing his gun around, but Lieutenant Ballard, with surprising speed, closed in on him and wrestled the gun away.

"Well," Bruno said, "what's this? What's the Coast Guard doing here? What's this business with guns and pushing people around? Mind telling me what's going on, lieutenant?" Bruno was the calmest person in the room.

Chris thought Lieutenant Ballard looked suddenly under strain, as if he'd gotten himself into something he wasn't sure of and now didn't know how to get out gracefully. Then he saw the lieutenant's chin come out, his sharp features turn marble hard, and he said, "Two men chased Yeoman George and his dog in here. Those men were carrying guns. We'd like to know what it's all about."

"Well, lieutenant, it's very simple." Bruno was completely calm and at ease. "Your Yeoman George, as you call him, came in here with this brute of a dog and demanded money. I've been threatened with guns, knives and other assorted weapons, but never with a dog. That's a new one. These two city detectives saw what was happening through the window and came in to help me out. They've been in here a number of times."

"That's not true." Jennie's brown eyes were snapping angrily. "It's just as I told you, lieutenant. I was coming home from work and I saw these two men chase Chris and Mike in here. I saw their guns. They've been following Chris for days, trying to kill Mike."

"That's downright silly," Bruno said easily. "Why would these men want to kill a dog? Ask them, lieutenant."

The slender man pushed his glasses up on his nose and in the same calm voice Bruno had used said, "Lieutenant, aren't you a little out of your jurisdiction? This is a police matter. It has nothing to do with the Coast Guard. We're perfectly capable of handling this without any help from you and your men. So why don't you just run along."

Chris could see that the complete calm and reasonableness of Bruno and the glasses-wearing man had shaken Ballard badly. He'd gotten over his own shock of learning Bruno was head of the drug racket, and he said now to Ballard, "Lieutenant, Jennie's right. If these men are detectives, make them show you credentials. They're here to kill Mike. There's a contract out on him. I wanted to tell you this afternoon but you wouldn't listen." He drew a deep breath and rushed on knowing he was killing all his hopes and dreams and ambitions. "Mike found three packages of heroin in the post office. I got rid of them because I was afraid if I told you, you'd think I was mixed up in it too. That's why Bruno put out the contract on Mike and why these men are trying to kill him. When we ran in here to get away from them, Bruno ordered these men to get rid of me too."

Bruno exploded angrily, "Of all the crazy nonsense. This guy's a mile off base, lieutenant. This's a bakery, a big wholesale bakery. I'm a baker. Ask anybody.

Look around you, man. This bakery has been here for forty years."

Ballard's black eyes raked over the tiers of baked goods, and Chris could see decision hardening and sharpening his features. Then he said to Chris in a biting voice, "Nice try, yeoman, but it won't wash. You've been nothing but trouble to me ever since we started this program. I don't know what kind of mess you've got·yourself into, but you're not using me and the service to get yourself out. We're going to the base right now. Captain Wilson's going to want to talk to you."

Chris's eyes had been darting about the room and had been caught by a small, familiar-looking cardboard box about eight inches square lying in a corner. There was printing on the box in black, block square letters: M. C. Douglas, General Delivery. It was the same box, same printing and even name that Mike had knocked off one of the pie carts in the post office. He was so startled he didn't even hear Lieutenant Ballard's words. His mind was leaping ahead to a conclusion, and things were dropping into place like the pieces of a jigsaw puzzle. He began talking, even as his mind was sorting out and arranging the facts.

"Lieutenant," he said excitedly, "this bakery is the headquarters for a drug operation. The drugs are put into boxes here and taken to the post office. The post office is the drop where the pushers pick up the drugs in general delivery. But it comes from here. I can prove it. The drugs are hidden right here in this room."

158

Ballard's sharp features were hard as marble and his eyes hit Chris with almost physical force. "Yeoman," his voice was ominous, "you'd better start proving that right now."

"Just a minute." Bruno had lost his cool. His big face was flushed with anger. "This is a private place. You've got no right coming in here and taking over. You've got no jurisdiction here, lieutenant. This is no ship. Now I want you and your people out of here right now. And take this, this troublemaker and his dog with you. Understand?"

Lieutenant Ballard and his squad had been returning to the base from another fruitless search of a freighter when Jennie ran into the road and stopped them. He was disappointed frustrated and angry. This was the second failure in a row. Things were looking black for him and the drug-bust program He was in no mood to be challenged and ordered about by a fat baker with flour all over his arms and face.

He snapped, "If this is a bakery, you've nothing to worry about. But the charge has been made and with a certain amount of justification. We're going to check it out." He indicated to one of the coastguardsmen, "Get your dog out of the car and bring him in here."

Chris said without really thinking, "This is Mike's job, lieutenant. We uncovered this. He's got a right to hunt it down."

"And go through another of your comedy acts." Ballard motioned to the coastguardsman again. "Get your dog."

Before the man could move to obey, Chris leaned down, unsnapped the leash from Mike's collar and said, "Go find it, Mike. Go on." It was the worst kind of insubordination, but Chris figured he was already so deep in trouble it didn't matter.

Ballard yelled angrily, "Come back here. Come back here!"

It was not Chris's voice ordering him, so Mike paid no attention. He trotted happily down an aisle doing the job he'd been trained for, head high, ears snapping back and forth, black nose questing and separating all the mouth-watering scents in the room.

Everyone stopped to watch the progress of the dog. Chris moved partway down the aisle to be near him.

Mike trotted up one aisle and down the next, stopping often to sniff into a corner or at a box or a loaf of bread. He covered the bread section and found nothing. He started down an aisle of tempting-looking pastries. He stopped suddenly and reared on hind legs before a shelf of pies.

Chris immediately spotted the lemon meringue topping, shining diamond bright under the lights. He yelled frantically, "No, Mike! No! No!" Mike gave the pie cart a wistful look, licked his chops hungrily, then dropped back on all fours and went on. Halfway down the aisle, Mike stopped again before a row of metal cans. His tail was waving, his head high and ears pricked forward. He reared up against the second shelf, nudged a round can off the shelf and began shoving it along the floor as he tried to bite into the metal.

Ballard, followed by Chris, strode down to the dog and picked up the can. He pried off the lid and looked at a round cake neatly packed in wax paper. He grunted disgustedly, "First it's lemon meringue pie. Now it's fruitcake."

Chris was studying the cake. It had cracked completely across the top and down the side. He remembered the fruitcakes his aunt made for Christmas. They were sticky and moist. Such a fall would not have cracked them.

Mike kept rearing up and whining and sniffing at the can. Chris said, "Lieutenant, that cake . . ." Before Ballard could object, he reached out and lifted the cake from the can and broke it in half. The inside was hollowed out. It was packed with a cellophane package of white powdery material.

Ballard grabbed the bag, ripped it open and tasted the powder. He reached for another can, opened it, broke the cake and found a second bag. He called to the guardsmen watching Bruno and the two men. "Hold those people right there. We've found something." He looked at Chris, his sharp features gone suddenly slack with surprise. There were a dozen cans, all alike, in the neat row. He said in a curiously tense voice, "Open another. Take that one on the end."

Chris opened the can, broke the cake and found another bag of powder.

Ballard strode down the aisle to Bruno, waving the white bags. Bruno was talking loudly even before the lieutenant got to him, "I don't know a thing about that stuff. I'm the night baker here. That's all. Just the night baker."

Ballard was in complete command of the situation now. "You're some baker, all right. We'll check that out. And we'll check out your detective friends. Take them out to the car," he instructed his men, "and don't let them get away. We'll pick up the rest of these cake boxes."

The coastguardsmen started to herd the men into the outer restaurant part when the street door opened and Captain Quinlan came in, seabag over his shoulder. He took in the scene and said to Bruno, "You're busy. I'll see you later," and turned to leave.

Mike let go a blood-curdling growl and before Chris could stop him, charged into the room, leaped on the retreating captain's back and fastened his teeth in the seabag. Mike's solid hundred pounds drove the captain to his knees. He twisted around and tried to jerk the seabag from Mike's jaws, but the dog hung on and began shaking the bag. Again the drawstring ripped open and dirty clothes spilled across the floor—and something else—a great number of plastic bags filled with a sugary white substance.

Everything happened at once. Lieutenant Ballard pounced on one of the bags. Captain Quinlan scrambled to his feet and turned to run. A coastguardsman leveled his gun at him and said sharply, "I wouldn't." The captain backed against the counter like a cornered animal. Chris grabbed the raging Mike, cuffed his ears and told him to be still.

162

Lieutenant Ballard looked at the plastic bag in his hands, at the empty seabag, the packages strewn across the floor. His eyes bored into Captain Quinlan and he said in the quietest voice Chris had ever heard him use, "Your tug brought the freighter in tonight. We didn't find the heroin because somebody on the freighter threw it over the rail, down to the tug before we went aboard—threw it to you, captain."

"You can't prove that," Captain Quinlan said hoarsely.

"I don't have to. It came out of your seabag."

Captain Quinlan looked at Lieutenant Ballard, then at Bruno and then at his seabag lying on the floor and last at the packages of heroin that had spilled from it. He licked his lips and a kind of pallor came up through the deep tan of his cheeks, and he said, "All I did was deliver it. I didn't have anything to do with anything else."

"Shut up," Bruno snapped. "They can't prove a thing."

Captain Quinlan ran on as if he hadn't heard, "You said it'd be easy. No problems. You lied to me. They've got us. They've got us dead to rights. Look at that stuff on the floor, man. And they found those phony cakes. What do you mean, they can't prove it."

Bruno ran a hand across his fat face. He was sweating. He opened his mouth to say something, then closed it without a word.

Ballard said, "Take them out to the car. I'll be along."

Captain Quinlan was the last to go. He looked at Jennie and Jennie looked back at him. Neither spoke. Then the captain turned and walked out.

Lieutenant Ballard said to Jennie, "He's your father, isn't he? I'm sorry."

Tears were running down Jennie's cheeks, but she asked, "What will they do to him? Will he go to jail?"

"I imagine so. After all, he was delivering drugs."

"For long?" Jennie asked.

"That depends on the judge."

Chris went to Jenny and put an arm around her. "Everything's going to be all right," he said. "Don't worry."

"It's definitely going to be all right," Lieutenant Ballard said. He was feeling good. He'd found the drugs he was after, and it looked as if he'd broken the back of the local drug ring. He said to Chris, "I'll talk to Captain Wilson first thing in the morning. You'll get your rating restored, and I guarantee you'll be back on the drug-bust program. You can move back to the base, too."

"I can't keep Mike on the base, sir," Chris said. "And Jennie and I have plans. I'd like to stay where I am, close to her."

"Of course," Ballard agreed.

There was a crash from the back room. All three ran in to see what had happened. Mike had knocked one of the pies off the shelf and was standing in the middle of it, happily lapping up the filling. He looked up, tail waving, face split in a happy dog grin. Lemon meringue was spread from the tip of his black nose to his brown eyes.

"Mike!" Chris started forward, but Lieutenant Ballard caught his arm. "Easy, sailor." He smiled. "He's earned it. The whole pie."